The Evolve Fertility Series

by Beth Alderman, MD, MPH

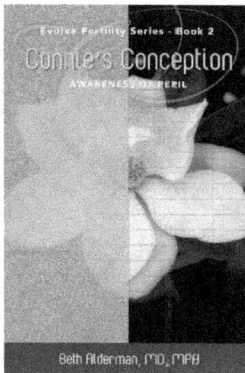

Melissa's Match

GREAT SOCIETY

Book One of the
Evolve Fertility Series

Beth Alderman, MD, MPH

LIVING FUTURE BOOKS • ASHLAND, OREGON

Melissa's Match: Great Society
by Beth Alderman, MD, MPH
© 2019 FutureMedicine, LLC
www.LivingFutureBooks.com

For related online courses visit
www.LivingFutureCourses.com

Editor: Julie Clayton
Cover Art: BruceBayard.com
Book Design: BookSavvyStudio.com

Library of Congress Control Number: 2019934973
ISBN: 978-1-7321110-1-1

First Edition
Printed in the United States of America

Contents

To Rhoda

Whoever fails to become light is a source of darkness.
—THE GOSPEL OF THOMAS (24)

1

Orientation Day

Melissa's parents stop their land boat in the busy street in front of Blackwood Hall, which will be her home for the next year at least. It is early afternoon. Melissa gets out of the back seat holding her possessions in a cardboard box, and her parents, intimidated by Chicago's noise and traffic, drive away back to Peoria, taking her childhood with them. She stares up at the tall, narrow building with its gray stone gothic façade and feels out of place. She knew college would be different, but didn't realize that every little thing would be unfamiliar, from the smell of the street to the manners of the other students entering the arched front door. She puts on a brave face and follows them into the first floor common room with a smile.

To her surprise, the common room has handsome, classic furniture that sets a formal but friendly tone. It is empty. She glimpses a student walking briskly up the stairs and follows to the third floor, which is also empty, and finds her room. It is a suite that has two rooms that share a bath. The one with the number on the door has a kitchenette and small dining table at the front, as well as a sofa. The décor is plain, and a bit shabby, but not entirely colorless. She goes to the far room and puts her few things in the closet. Then she makes her single bed and puts a towel on the rack in the bathroom. With butterflies in her stomach, she leaves to register for classes.

By two o'clock in the afternoon, she has completed her registration checklist and has her fall timetable of classes. She reaches the rain-washed quadrangle for the formal orientation of new students just in time to find the auditorium in Hutchinson Commons, take a red, plush seat in the back row, and admire the carved detail of the dark wood interior. After announcements, the dean, a gaunt, intense man with a fetlock of gray hair and a pince-nez, takes the podium. He welcomes the incoming students to the University of Chicago, and tells them they are the crème de la crème of their graduating classes. He exhorts them to pursue excellence for themselves and for the honor of this Harvard of the Midwest, of which they will soon be proud alumni. It is heady stuff. Her anticipation rises. She can hardly wait for classes to begin.

Melissa walks back to her dorm room alone, this time with a heartwarming sense of belonging. Her imagination fills the blank year ahead with solemn but sublime scholarly pursuits. She feels welcome, open, engaged and happy. She is even undaunted by meeting her roommate, April, who comes from a farm down-state—a highly profitable industrial one that has given her an air of privilege. April has brought a trunk full of stylish clothing—and turns up her nose at Melissa's working class past. April's deep-set brown eyes and high breasts are set off by shiny auburn hair that stops above her narrow waist. She looks beautiful in the way of a Modigliani painting, with a manner that is tense, reserved, and disapproving—and presses her lips together like a model in a teen magazine. Melissa doesn't know how to put April at ease, and right now is mainly concerned about keeping her cool and finding her own place in this strange and wonderful menagerie of students from all over the country. She goes through the shared bathroom to put away her coat and brush her hair. Looking in the mirror behind the hall door that opens into her room, she feels self-conscious about her wide shoulders and hips; muscular legs; and the square jaw, round cheeks, bug-eyed glasses, and ready smile that dominate her face. Though they barely spoke, April has already remarked on how pale Melissa's eyes are, and how her dark eyebrows and lashes suggest that the golden tone and red highlights of her once-blond hip-length hair will soon be gone.

Melissa takes a deep breath, takes the lid off her eager curiosity, and goes to April's room to suggest that they go downstairs together for new student orientation to the dorm. They descend in silence to the common room and scan the group of dorm mates spread out on the sofas and couches around the heavy oak coffee table near the fireplace. April takes a seat in an armchair, and Melissa sits on the floor beside it, eyeing the softshelled and hardshelled students from the east coast in their fancy jeans and feeling a small fire of inner joy at the expansion of her world.

Professor and Mrs. Weitzman, the Resident Masters, emerge from their ground floor apartment and enter the common room. The student in the biggest armchair gives up his seat to the Resident Master, while his wife finds a place on a couch. The students stop whispering. Melissa's anticipation rises. She is excited about the sophisticated wine and cheese parties mentioned in the college brochure. The Professor looks at the students sternly, raises his deliberate, German-accented voice, and intones impassively, "You shoult neffer go out ahfter dark."

Melissa is not sure how to take this. Weitzman's continental manner is hard for her to read. His hands cup the wooden armrests rigidly; his lips move just enough in his pear-shaped face to reveal short, blackened teeth; and his black suit and narrow black tie remind her of a financier trying to appear trustworthy. She glances at the faces of other students and fails to find clues, but the short, plump Mrs. Weitzman tells Melissa what she needs to know. Warm and glowing at first, the Resident Mistress grows as still and grim as a figure in a wax museum. Tension covers Melissa's skin like a wetsuit of mistrust.

"Bubala," Mrs. Weitzman chimes in, adjusting her antique suit and amber bouffant with one hand and squeezing her handkerchief with the other, "tell them about the Golden Rectangle."

"*Main tayere vaib—*"

"On every corner, there are the white safety telephones. You lift the receiver and a car will come to you," Mrs. Weitzman interjects. She explains that the University Police patrol Hyde Park within an area called the Golden Rectangle, and that the students should not leave its limits.

Dr. Weitzman continues to explain matter-of-factly that the leaders of the Blackwood Rangers street gang, who were involved in minor disorganized crimes, are being released from Joliet State Penitentiary and will be returning to Blackwood Street armed and dangerous. The state locked them up with professional, organized criminals who gave them an education in perpetration; now the University will have to lock them out. The Administration doesn't want any more students to be thrown out of windows and killed, as happened the year before.

A photographer who has been snapping pictures of the group pauses, lowers his camera, and scowls. Apparently, he doesn't like what he hears. Neither does Melissa. She looks away from the students' unhappy faces and sees, through the picturesque leaded glass windows, a swirl of brown leaves. She is nostalgic for the elegant monasticism that she read into the fake gothic architecture designed for the Columbian Exposition. She realizes now that it is a prison, and that its heavy furnishings, which seemed stately, are institutional.

"The *grits* girl," Mrs. Weitzman urges with a wave of her handkerchief. "Talk to her."

Dr. Weitzman sighs heavily and intones, "Some of you are from big cities and know how to behafe. Some of you are from small towns and will have to learn quickly."

The Professor turns to April, who was recruited through a new university program called the Grass Roots Talent Search, that students call "grits." April flushes as he tells her that she must walk purposefully and briskly up the middle of the street, avoid eye contact with strangers, and give a wide berth to any shrub or wall that might conceal an assailant. She must also keep cash on hand at all times to pay off a mugger. If she were broke, the mugger might shoot or stab her.

Melissa feels the warmth of intellectual passion ebb and the chill of fear rise. She is surprised to feel her roommate relax. Apparently April expects society to fail. Melissa doesn't. She is shocked. She can't reconcile the afternoon's orientation with this one. A brilliant faculty of Nobel prize winners can't create a safe community? Are they really fit to teach? And how can students study well if they have to fear for their lives?

Sarah, a girl from Baltimore with long blonde hair, raises her hand and echoes Melissa's thoughts ironically, "The dean told us to pursue academic excellence. How do we do that without going to the library?"

Nervous laughter simmers around the room, reviving the photographer's interest. All eyes turn to Weitzman, who replies, "You must study in your roomss."

When all the students begin whispering at once, he glowers and adds irritably, "If you must go to ze campuss ahfter dark, be sure to go in a gwroup."

"What about dinner?" Melissa asks. "We need to eat something."

"Ze store arount ze corner iss closed. You shoult have bought groceries earliah."

The message is clear: Weitzman will take care of theory, and they will take care of practical matters. On that unsatisfying note, he and his wife disappear into their rooms, and the students disperse. Some go directly to the stairway and ascend to their rooms. Others linger.

Melissa stays where she is, trying to shake off the tension. It isn't easy. She was raised on fear. She still feels her knees pressed into the polished wooden floor beneath her third grade desk, where she hid during nuclear war drills. Her young soul over-flows with stories of World War II, the Cold War, and the War in Vietnam. Ever since she can remember, her elders have been recruiting ever more enemies to make sense of their precious patrimony of fear. She is not surprised that they would blindly collude with the desperate and destitute to create the antipathy required to sustain it.

Fear is as familiar as air, but disappointment is not. Melissa swallows her sadness at having lost faith in rationality already, before the first class of the first year. The dean made her believe that she could trust the university. She had faith, for a few wonderful hours, that she would have the chance to push back the frontiers of knowledge rather than only work off personal fears of poverty and helplessness. She blames the brilliant minds that brought the world the bomb, some of who still teach here, and who did not put on sackcloth and ashes, or sing out a purifying *mea culpa* after Fat Man and Little Boy vaporized Japanese cities. They have not moved on. They have no idea how to live in peace.

Melissa notices that the sun has sunk, leaving the room in shadow. She gets up and pulls the chain of a pole lamp behind her. Several more lights go on in quick succession, filling the room with a welcome glow. Sarah materializes at Melissa's side and says, "I thought gloom and doom would talk all night. Let's get a group together for dinner."

Melissa smiles brightly. Her mood is buoyed by Sarah's generous irreverence, which pierces the shroud of humorlessness. "Great idea!"

This is the first time Sarah has been easy and familiar, and Melissa is glad of it. Earlier in the day, she noticed Sarah's purposeful, self-possessed and business-like manner with the faculty and staff, and took her for an older transfer student. She is poised and fit, with heavy-lidded eyes and lips brightened by a lively, sometimes sly, smile. Her magnetism delights Melissa. They have soon gathered others to make up a group.

Ten minutes later, Melissa and six other new students spill out onto the sidewalk and start north up Blackwood Avenue. In front are Sarah and a tall, skinny raven-haired boy named John, who is wearing a black beret and leading the way.

Melissa takes to John's easy-going, unpretentious manner. She tries not to think about whether or not she finds him attractive, but can't help it, and can't decide. She is put off by his long sharp features, acne scars, and impossibly narrow hips, but is drawn to his ease, light grace, and resonant baritone. Finally, she is won over by the humor in his intense green eyes. As they walk on, she begins to feel safe in his company.

Soon, though, they pass a black man in a beret, whose perfect features are spoiled by a hostile gaze and long scar down the left cheek. Melissa is shocked when he runs his eyes brazenly over her body. She is even more surprised when John nods to the stranger in a friendly way. She suspects the nod was silly rather than savvy, and falls back to walk with Doug and Zeke, who are bringing up the rear.

Doug, a hulking, freckled man in a bush hat and trench coat who grew up in the southern suburbs, is half cool cat and half clown. He passes time by needling Zeke, a mousy physics major from Pittsburgh with a frizzy ponytail and an obtrusive awareness of his own brilliance. They are like a bad comedy duo.

"Hey, Einstein, let's get a keg and find some hot chicks."

"You look like the kind of person who would have time for that sort of thing."

"Hey, that thing on the back of your head looks like a mouse on a rubber band."

"Did they let you out of some kind of mental facility?"

Melissa turns her attention to April, who is walking just ahead with Alan. April, who was overawed by the dean, and alarmed and embarrassed by the Resident Master, is enjoying her walk with Alan. He is giving her tips on city life, along with a monologue about life on Long Island. In appearance, Alan has the same brown eyes, narrow face, and slender form as April, but he is taller, short-haired and hirsute. It doesn't take Melissa long to see that Alan is showing off his masculinity, or that April is taken with him.

As they walk, the gathering night drains warmth and color from the air, and Melissa grows uneasy. Cars speed by frequently and impersonally. Each pedestrian is walking a big, unfriendly dog. Sodium street lamps switch on, bathing the street in eerie, yellow-orange twilight. The trees are stately and the mansions impressive, but unkempt lawns, ostentatious burglar alarms, and drawn shades turn this seeming island of affluence into a big-city slum.

When the group reaches 55th Street, and is about to cross out of the Golden Rectangle, Melissa rushes to the front again to speak with John. As they dart between onrushing cars, Sarah falls back, and Melissa keeps up with John's long stride. "Where are you taking us?"

"Beaulieu's." John explains that he ate there with his family the day before, when they brought him down from Steven's Point, Wisconsin.

Melissa worries when they reach 53rd Street, a strip crowded by down-at-the-heels pedestrians and busy with rust-spotted cars trailing acrid smoke.

John stops in front of a brightly lit storefront with glass windows that are frosted at the bottom and decorated with gold-edged script that says, "Beaulieu's Café, See your food, Eat your food." Inside, a single room glistening with white tile, chrome, and glass is filled with three rows of tables, customers of all descriptions, and a cafeteria line at the back.

"It's not what I expected," Melissa says to John.

"What did you expect?"

"Some kind of French restaurant, I guess."

John raises an eyebrow, smiles crookedly, and leads the way inside. Entering is like turning the volume of a radio all the way up. They plunge into the clatter of dishes and utensils, the scraping of chairs, the crying of a toddler, and broken waves of raucous laughter coming from a table of exotic young men who turn out to be from the University's International House. All are immersed in the tangy scent of okra and a strong aroma of chicken fat.

Melissa is glad to have been to a cafeteria before. She knows what to do. She follows Alan, April, and John to the back, where they take fiberglass trays from a stack on the right and pull them along a slide to the hot food service counter in the middle. Behind the counter stands an intimidating, middle-aged black woman with the body of a fertility fetish, whose nametag says "Miss Taylor." Melissa stops to stare at the food, perplexed by the unfamiliar offerings on display in huge, stainless steel basins.

"Black-eyed peas, chit'lins, grits, turnip greens, sweet potato pie ..." John rattles off the names of the foods, which would help if Melissa knew which was which.

Miss Taylor drops a fresh basin of succotash into its warmer with a crash, raising an enormous cloud of steam. When it clears, she narrows her eyes at the ceiling, points at Melissa with a huge serving spoon, and says, "What you doing, girl? The food be over here."

Anxious and eager to placate the woman, Melissa replies, "I don't know what to order."

"It don't make no never mind to me, but you better have the special unless you f'in to stand there all night." Miss Taylor shouts something at the open kitchen door behind her, raising a laugh at the front.

"Okay, um, I'll, uh, have the special, then. Thanks."

Miss Taylor slaps several spoonfuls onto a plate and tosses it onto the display shelf. "Nex'!"

As Melissa takes her plate, John turns to her, points to the till ahead, and says in a hushed voice, "That's Jerome Beaulieu, the owner."

Melissa steps out of line to peek at Jerome, a middle-aged man in a large Afro. He is wearing a stark uniform that glows white against his dark skin. She can see that he has appeal. She watches him, wondering if its source is intelligence, graciousness, kindness, humor, or spontaneity. She decides on charisma. Melissa is relieved to find, when she reaches the till, that he crosstalks patiently even when she fumbles her wallet. She feels welcome. By the time she and John push tables together to hold their group, she is feeling better about her slowness and lack of city street smarts.

When the group settles down to eat and talk, however, her tentative ease evaporates. The motley group has little in common. Some are even eager to find points of contention. Her Lutheran manners balk at this recreational discord. Nothing here will ever feel like home, she realizes with a pang. Home is gone forever. She will have to adapt.

Melissa watches the friends that fate chose for her and tries to grok them by using the stereotypes from her high school. She can't. Sarah looks the slut, but is too opinionated and smart to be an object. April seems like a goody two-shoes, but can't be one in a confluence of cultures with no agreed on idea of right or good. Zeke lacks social graces and humor, but his fund of knowledge is too broad and deep to be contained by the notion of a nerd. John, who has street smarts, and Alan, who is Jewish, fall entirely outside the range of her experience. Doug is the only one she can categorize. He is the class clown.

Exhausted by the hyper-attentiveness of newness, and short on patience, Melissa expects to lose her cool before anyone else, but Doug beats her to it. He starts trouble by teasing April about the Grass Roots Talent Search, and explaining that the university started it to crush the hard-boiled activists from New York who had enraged the Administration by taking over its building in 1968. The university then rejected its urban feeder schools, and turned to more tractable talent from the rural Midwest. Doug sums this up with, "They wanted hicks who were easy to control."

April's eyes redden.

Alan retorts, "Do you mean easier to control or more conservative?"

"What's the difference?" Doug replies smartly, his manner shifting from goofy to sharp.

"Well, I'm from the city and I don't support anti-war radicals."

"Are you saying you support the war in Vietnam?" Melissa asks incredulously. Hardly anyone admits to that now, in 1972, when only the most deluded see the war as justifiable or winnable.

"Yes, I am."

The group recoils, with the exception of April. "We have to fight the communist threat," she leans forward earnestly and whispers, "and criminals."

"Why aren't you over there now?" Melissa asks Alan pointedly.

"I don't think my talents are best used in that way."

"Nixon prefers black men as cannon fodder," Zeke interjects coldly.

A hush falls over nearby tables. Jerome glances their way.

John says sharply, "I think that's immoral, don't you?"

"Morality is a matter of opinion."

"Hurting people is bad," Melissa asserts stubbornly.

"Ergo Doug is bad." Zeke looks at April, who blushes.

"Stick it in your ear, Zeke," Doug mutters sulkily.

"Doug—" Sarah begins. She stops abruptly. They hear a commotion outside. Footfalls approach fast. They hear a report like a car backfiring, a heavy thud, and a loud groan. Melissa turns to see a silhouette slide down the frosted glass of the window, leaving a dark streak and a tiny hole.

Melissa has never experienced anything like this. Back home, troublemakers used knives and chains. Looking around uncertainly, she sees a shadow pass over the faces of the locals. Miss Taylor's mask-like expression turns grim and blank. April is transfixed. Sarah says quietly, "Oh, Christ."

Melissa can't believe someone was shot not fifteen feet away. In Peoria, everyone knows where the trouble spots are, and most who choose to do so can avoid them. Here, trouble has followed them to this public place. Worse, the shot hit home and no one is doing anything about it. She feels a surge of panic. She knows that Dr. Weitzman would tell her to look straight ahead and avoid eye contact, but her feelings and judgment rebel against this cold-bloodedness. "Shouldn't we go outside and see if anyone needs help?"

Alan replies authoritatively, "That would be too dangerous."

Zeke, Doug, and Sarah remain still, as does April, who is staring at Alan.

"We can't just sit here while someone bleeds to death!"

"Chances are the police shot a criminal," Alan asserts irritably.

Melissa looks at John. He nods slightly. They both rise cautiously from their seats.

This is the immortal moment that Melissa will remember long after the sound of the gunshot has faded from her mind, long after the fear has left her soul. While the helpless April, the self-preserving Alan, the rational Zeke, the cheeky Doug, and the city sophisticate Sarah all sit and talk, John stands. He is ready to take responsibility, ready to act, ready to join with her in acting for the good of all regardless of the danger and in spite of the fact that he is not sure just what to do. In this little microcosm of the Ivory Tower—of American society—he is the one she would trust with her life. While the others look out at the world and see only themselves, he engages. She sees this now, on day one, but it will take her a lifetime to comprehend it.

The moment ends when Sarah, who is seated facing the till, says calmly, "Let Jerome handle it. He already called for help."

A long moment later, blue lights flash outside. John and Melissa look at each other with relief and sit down. They hear feet scuff, car doors slam, engines rev and recede. Melissa pushes away her plate; she closes her eyes and feels the hairline cracks in her sense of peace and safety enlarge and extend. She wonders if she will ever be able to repair them.

When she opens her eyes again, she notices a rangy black man in a frayed gabardine suit pacing inside the window, his nostrils flaring, his breath quick and deep, his face animated by agitated pleasure. He is thrilled. A student in jeans with wide-set eyes and wiry red hair joins him. Melissa recognizes the boy as Thomas, a freshman from Blackwood, who must have come in with another group. Thomas and the man talk excitedly in low voices. They seem to be salving some kind of inner discontent with this obscene slice of violence.

Melissa hears a soft voice say, "Jet? Jet?" A young boy stops at her elbow to hawk a handful of small magazines. A tiny brass bell at the top of the front door tinkles and a lean man in a white shirt, black tie, and black pants enters to refresh the stack of Black Muslim papers that sits on a metal stand inside the front door. Soon after, the din returns to its usual pitch and volume, and the group gets ready to leave.

On the way home, Zeke launches into a polysyllabic monologue about Noam Chomsky, rousing wisecracks from Doug and outbursts from Alan. Sarah and Alan comfort April as best they can. John and Melissa walk side-by-side chatting about life back home, having recognized each other as kindred spirits. Others soon seek John out as if they, too, valued his calm integrity. Before long, Melissa finds herself walking with Zeke instead, who has much to say when he is not overwhelmed by a group.

Back at Blackwood, April closes herself in the bathroom, leaving Melissa to ruminate on the ivory tower and the surrounding ghetto, each of which is sure to teach them very different, and very conflicted, ways of growing up.

2

Study

idterms are over and Sarah has all her grades back. She has not done as well as expected: In the pecking order of her study group, her expected GPA is fifth of six. At least she is keeping up with the overachievers who keep her motivated and on track. She pulls her backpack straps forward to stop her books from pulling her backward, and lags strategically behind Doug, who likes to needle her. Sarah looks at the gray sky and brown trees of 57th Street and misses the beauty of Hyde Park at the beginning of fall, and the ease of the first few weeks of classes. Still, she is glad that she didn't go to school in California, where warm weather and lush nature might have drawn her out of doors, or her social life might have gotten out of control. Here, she can stay in the dorm in the evening and visit friends when gregariousness gets the better of discipline.

Fortunately, Sarah chose her classes well. As Doug, Alan, and John turn toward 59th Street and their Western Civilization course with Professor Weitzman, she is glad that she has a less Socratic and more entertaining professor; when April leaves to go to Art History, Sarah is glad to be going with Melissa to their 10 a.m. Shakespeare class. Melissa can be relied on for competence and support, and always has Sarah's back; she isn't much fun, but can be counted on at any time of the day or night, and is often pensive and quiet in the morning, when Sarah is in no mood to chat. Sarah only needs to walk slowly enough to make sure that only the front seats are available.

When they ascend the dark creaking stairs in the far inner corner of the quadrangle, and enter the stark and somewhat shabby classroom darkened by the hospital building across the street, Sarah's heart skips a beat as she takes a seat in the front and waits breathlessly for Professor Henshaw to read. A few minutes after ten, when all the students have taken seats, he makes his entrance, taking a last drag of his cigarette before pulling it out of his mouth with a flourish, rounding the desk and sitting on top of it with his feet dangling. He tosses his long brown hair behind the collar of his corduroy suit and adjusts his well-worn jeans and wire-rimmed glasses. If not for his early crow's feet he would look like a graduate student. Picking up the book on his desk and opening it on his lap with one hand, he stubs out his cigarette with the other and begins to read Hamlet's graveyard scene.

Sarah thrills to his voice—the rhythm and intonation, the English accent and portentous pauses. It is like being sung awake, especially when he stares at her breasts, which arouses her. He has already seduced her with his mute appeal; the only question is whether to sleep with him or not. Back home, the answer would be clear: yes. Here, she is not sure. Instead of being perceived as adventurous, she might be seen as shallow, or worse, as having poor taste and bad judgment. She glances at Melissa, who is staring at her blank notebook with a blank expression, and decides to float the idea at lunch.

Later, after buying sandwiches at the bookstore, they sit in the snack room down the stairs from Harper Library with April and Anne, a girl from the dorm. Anne is a short, stooped, furtive-looking sophmore with curly mahogany hair, freckled skin and a blunt way of speaking. She already has a reputation for always wearing a wool hat with the earflaps turned up, for disliking women, and for making friends with, and then for sleeping with, a different man every Friday. Word on the street has it that she was raped before her teens. The rumors aren't all true; for one thing, she has women friends, one of whom is Sarah, who makes a point of knowing everyone's business without volunteering opinions about what she knows. In that, Sarah is the opposite of Melissa, who forms opinions about everything but doesn't pry. After they have eaten, and before they go, Sarah looks around at the other two tables and three snack machines, and apparently decides that it is noisy and chaotic enough that she can gossip freely.

"So what do you think of Henshaw?" she asks Melissa.

"He's all right," Melissa says neutrally. "You seem to like him."

"I love his voice! The way he reads!"

"I've heard you have to sleep with him to get an A," April says with disgust.

"He's a creep," Anne says. When he refused to sleep with her on the grounds that it would be sex abuse, she took offense, and now contributes to his bad reputation when she can. "He's old, he smells, he'll sleep with anyone, and he doesn't even care about English. They shouldn't let him teach."

"I have to admit I don't like the way he looks at us, and he doesn't teach us much—except by bad example," Melissa says.

"Alan says the guys say Henshaw thinks with his you-know-what. They have no respect for him."

Sarah is glad she brought it up. She turns to gather her things and go up to Harper Library to study, but Melissa stops her by asking, "What do you think of Neal?"

"Neal the Nihilist?" Anne asks sardonically.

"Neal the atheist teacher of religion," April says.

"Comparative religions," Melissa says. "I suppose he can't take sides."

"Faith is faith. He doesn't have it. He doesn't get it. He isn't qualified to teach it," April says.

"I've heard that he's a former Catholic who hates religion," Sarah says.

"Why would he teach it?"

"He knows a lot about it," Sarah says.

"From the outside," April interjects.

"The atheists and scientists seem to like him," Sarah says.

"Do you?"

"I like teachers who love what they teach and give us its best so we can love it too. He seems to hate religion."

"He's Jewish and he blames the holocaust on religion," Anne says. "I think he's sort of making a case against it."

"Trying it in class?" Sarah asks.

"Trying to work it out," Anne says in a raw voice that reminds the others that she, too, struggles with invisible wrongs.

"Well, I wish him luck," Melissa says, "but I wish I hadn't taken his class!"

Sarah stands. A clean-cut, middle-aged graduate student takes her seat. Harper and the snack area are in the business school, but few affiliated with the school linger in the afternoon or evening. The four girls enter the library through security, where a bored work-study student is filling in for the elderly man in a cardigan who usually looks inside their backpacks and pats them down.

April turns left at the desk and left again to go into the cozy conversation pit where Alan and Doug usually sprawl on the bright blue prism-shaped floor pillows and read. Anne goes off to sit on the floor in a corner of the stacks, and Melissa heads over to sit with John at an otherwise empty study table in the great hall at the heart of Harper Library. Sarah sits in a carrel nearby, but soon finds her math homework doesn't sustain her interest and begins eavesdropping on Melissa and John, who, like most people, intrigue her. They seem to be the stereotypical Midwesterners that she had hoped to meet, and yet so unalike that she cannot see what it is that they like about each other.

John is brilliant, deep, street smart, and strong—and in this group that straddles the street life of the city and the heady life of the classroom, he is emerging as the natural leader. But he is quiet, and keeps his thoughts to himself to the point that Sarah cannot say whether he is an open book, or is reserved and secretive, or is not to be trusted. She allows his leadership, but keeps a close eye on him. Melissa, on the other hand, is a straight-shooting straight arrow who keeps her own compass and counsel and, while she can keep a secret and would never betray a friend, knows and speaks her mind freely and to a fault.

"I love when the light comes in that way," Melissa says, pointing to the sunbeams that are penetrating the high arched windows of the great hall, and illuminating the stone and dark wood ceiling two stories above.

John looks, smiles distractedly, and goes back to penciling out responses to his higher-level math homework. After a pause, he sighs and says, "It's modeled after Cambridge."

"Wasn't that a monastery at one time?"

"The church handled education back then."

"Neal would be horrified," Melissa replies. After a shorter pause she asks tentatively, "Don't you feel like all this studying is changing you?"

John laughs under his breath. "You mean making me dull?"

"No. I mean I can't remember how I saw the world before I got here. It's like trying to remember what I thought before I could read, or speak—or before last week. It's like I'm a *tabula rasa* each morning, and I dream my way into a new world each night. Do you know what I mean?"

John looks up at her and says, "I think so. Once you get something, you can't not get it, and can't remember not getting it. It changes your perspective."

"Yes, exactly. It can even change your expectations and your responses to experience. It makes you a different person."

"If it's important, yeah. It can. That's why we're here, isn't it?"

"I think a lot of people are here to get a degree for success and security."

"It doesn't have to be either or."

"I hope not," Melissa says doubtfully.

Sarah smiles at their earnestness. At first she thought of them as provincial, or small town, or poor, and they are, but there is something else in them, something she envies. They have an inner wealth that most people lack, a habit of observing and refining the mind for the purpose of self-cultivation. They are open-minded, unpretentious, and possessed of the humble confidence and quiet courage to turn toward what they do not know in order to make something from the void that most people shun. They are seekers who are always finding, explorers who are always delighting in the smallest discovery and looking forward to the next. No wonder they have such a tolerance for endless study; they seem to like it, and to take breaks only in order to be better able to study more. And yet not quite, because they seek outside experience in the same way, visiting various neighborhoods and attending distant cultural events. And so, to outsiders, they appear as nerds; and to insiders, as keepers of the flame of human knowledge.

Later, when Sarah has gotten through her math and they are walking home, she notices April's tailored wool coat, and smoothes out her own. Doug loves to make fun of April's closet, which is filled with fine clothes that no student would wear, and is also color-coded and strictly ordered by warmth and style and annotated on index cards. April doesn't fit in, nor does Sarah. Doug has mocked her coat as well. He sometimes implies that she is showing off, or is shallow, or—and this worries her—will "freeze her cookies" when winter comes. She has been walking with Doug, who is moping about something, and seems about to take it out on her, so she is glad to join Melissa and April and to raise the subject of the coat.

"I'm thinking I need a new coat."

"Why?" Melissa asks. "That one looks fine."

"Doug says it isn't warm enough."

"I need one, too." April says. "When I bought my clothes I always had a ride."

"I like to wear camouflage," Melissa says. "I'm going to get more winter clothes from the army navy store."

"Why?" April laughs. "You'll look like a bum."

"Good. I want to look like I'm not worth mugging or hitting on."

"You don't want a boyfriend?"

"Two-thirds of our class is male. The admissions office does that on purpose because they think we're here to get our M.R.S. degree. That means the homely men—which is most of them, let's face it—never get sex and always want it. I'm in science, which means I feel the pressure all the time. If I looked like either of you I'd have to fight them off with a stick! That's why I want to dress like a lumberjack."

"They'll think you're a lesbian," says Sarah.

"They'll call you a dog," says April.

"Good! As long as they don't *call* me!"

Melissa changes the subject to one that interests her more. "Have you noticed that our professors seem like they've never spoken to each other?"

"No," April says.

"What do you mean?" Sarah asks.

"Each seems to live in a different world, and to leave it to us to put those worlds together. I like jigsaw puzzles, but this one has too many gaps."

"They're each teaching in their own field," April says unhelpfully.

"That's what core courses are for—for giving us a broad base of knowledge. I think they work pretty well."

"Maybe that's the problem. I deferred a couple of those," Melissa sighs heavily.

"They say that a generalist knows less and less about more and more until she knows nothing about everything, and a specialist knows more and more about less and less until she knows everything about nothing. You can't win."

April says, "Everyone wants to be a specialist. That's where the good jobs are. That's where the money is."

"It seems more like everybody knows nothing. I mean, if a field is disconnected, it's useless, isn't it?"

"It's a bit extreme, I guess, but please tell me I don't have to take more science! I have very little aptitude for it," Sarah says.

"Everybody's different," April says.

"That's right—and *vive la difference!*"

When Sarah reaches the dorm she says, "I'm going to Regenstein tonight. Don't leave without me."

"Ditto," says April.

"Does this have anything to do with Alan?" Sarah asks, spooling out a pleasurable intonation of insinuation.

April blushes. Melissa suppresses a smile and says, "See you at the front door at six!"

When they meet downstairs later, and resume their walk-and-talk, Melissa asks, "Why Regenstein Library?"

"I've had enough of the dorm, for now," Sarah replies. She entertains her companions with character sketches of the students whose rooms she visits most often, leaving out Melissa and April's rooms. She describes Alan's room, with its unexpected Jimi Hendrix posters, rock album collection, and the electric guitar that he isn't allowed to play in the dorm; Doug's pigsty room, which she fears will draw cockroaches; the guys who play guitar badly but hope it will attract women anyway, and the classical guitarist who transports women with his playing but doesn't want to attract women; the women whose rooms look like antique stores or craft dens; and the women who keep hoping a man will knock. She avoids mentioning those who are depressed, or can't escape their family problems, like the New York tough guy whose father just gambled away his winter quarter tuition; or the closeted gay man who worked as a cocktail waiter in the summer and was fleeced by an older man who broke his heart. She wants to escape all the lonely hearts who have poured out woes that make her feel useless.

When they approach the rough cement building that houses the posh new library and resembles an irregular pile of building blocks—or, as Melissa says, a fortress—they divide into two groups, science and humanities, and when they reach the second floor, find separate study tables.

Every now and then Sarah takes a break and visits the science tables, where John presides by virtue of his mastery, Melissa sits opposite him by virtue of her fascination with their subjects, and Doug and Alan listen to the discussion and get as many extra homework pointers as they can. Zeke sometimes joins them but is usually too far ahead, as does Randall, who is here because he is a Jewish intellectual, but always runs behind because he is a gorgeous out-of-place Californian with an active sex life. When Sarah walks by she hears Melissa trying to explain physics by giving the example of a turn that she learned in ballet class. Sarah smiles to herself and feels sorry for Melissa for taking the boys' teasing badly, for being too traditionally and solicitously feminine to ignore their immature behavior or to show them the proper disrespect. It is by watching them that she realizes that John is a sleeper, a gentleman who looks out for Melissa's feelings graciously and kindly, and is reserved rather than a cold fish.

Later, when they are all walking home together, Sarah positions herself in front of Melissa and John so that she can hear their conversation. They are talking about the physics professor, who seems depressed when he talks about entropy and black holes, and seems to both of them to be the professor who is most like a surrogate parent, or a minister. He, and they, are in awe of the mysteries of the universe, and are best able to express wonder and amazement when contemplating the splendor and intricacy of creation. Finally, Melissa says, "We'll never be the same, will we? I wonder what we'll be like when we graduate."

"I don't know. I've been thinking about what you said earlier, about how what we're learning shifts our perspective, and our relation to everything. I think that's why the singularities—the one-time events like eating in Greektown or going to a play at Steppenwolf Theater—stand out so much."

"They do, don't they! It isn't just that we ignore routine. We change and we start over, and over—in our minds, but not in our social lives. We're still kids. Even some of our Profs seem like overgrown kids."

"Promise me we won't become academics! It would be like never leaving school!"

Sarah smiles as she realizes that Melissa and John think they are just friends. In their platonic innocence they have no idea what is coming, or how complicated it will be for all of them.

3

Motorcycle

Savoring the prospect of a wild ride to cap a long night in the library, Doug crams his books into his backpack, then stops abruptly. He is like a marathoner who, halfway to the finish line, realizes his water bottle is empty—he has forgotten to invite a chick to ride behind him on the bike. The female is an essential part of the fantasy. *Fuck!*

He can come up with a chick. Any chick will do. He looks at Melissa sitting across the big wooden study table by the central stairwell of Regenstein Library, putting the finishing touches on the calculus homework. She isn't exactly female. She does well in physics and never makes herself up. As quickly as a snap of the fingers, though, his rhetoric-ready mind arranges these facts into an argument that he can treat her like a gal pal or a dyke, and therefore cajole, threaten, or beg without losing face.

Doug says as offhandedly as he can manage, "Hey, want to go for a spin on my bike?"

Melissa looks up. Her eyebrows are knotted and her pupils are giving him the x-ray treatment, and he has the unpleasant feeling she can see what he is thinking. He fusses with his backpack zipper and glances at her surreptitiously. She puts away her books, shrugs her face, and says, "Why not? Physics is driving me nuts. We can crash for all I care."

When they reach Blackwood Hall, and put away their backpacks, Doug brings out his motorbike from a shed on the back alley. It is small and dented and lacks the style of a chopper, but it is his, and it runs. He straddles the bike with a sigh that blows away the cares of the day. He grasps the cold handlebars, grips the chassis between his eager thighs, and signals Melissa to get on. She hops on and sits as far back on the banana seat as possible.

Doug hands her the spare helmet. "You're going to fall off. Move up and hold on to me. Tight. You can put your hands anywhere you want."

"Doug! Eeew." Her hands touch his ribs gingerly, but she shifts her body a little farther back.

"Suit yourself. But lean in on the turns. If you don't, we'll go down."

Doug puts on his helmet, guns the farting engine, and squeals away with a lurch. He feels Melissa's arms encircle his waist, and her warm inner thighs grip his legs. She feels like a chick. As long as he can't see her, he can imagine that she is a real chick, one that wants a good time. When her body leans naturally into the turns, he relaxes, speeds up and lets the sharp breeze, exhilarating speed, and ever-present sense of hazard feed his fantasy of freedom.

Doug becomes a *voyageur*. In his mind, he is Leatherstocking, Sitting Bull, Robert Peary, Woody Guthrie, Jack Kerouac, Carlos Castenada, Evil Knievel, and most of all, Easy Rider. He is a young man fueled by hormones and urges he can't name, which he would think of in the crudest terms, if were he willing to think at all.

"What if it breaks down?" Melissa shouts in his ear.

"That's part of the fun," Doug replies glibly.

He speeds southward across the Midway, which students call the DMZ after the demilitarized zone in Vietnam. They speed through the grim decay of Woodlawn, where darkness favors the once fine, stone clad six-flats, the boarded up shops with twisted iron gates, and the vacant lots littered with broken glass.

"This is like Dresden after the war!" Melissa says when he makes a rolling stop at a deserted intersection.

Doug doesn't care to be reminded of Weitzman's constant references to World War II. He speeds away from the university's confining notions of living and into the kaleidoscope of potentiality beyond. He leaves behind the endless hours of sitting, concentrating, and calculating, leaning now into movement, aggression, and transgression. He defies humorless authority by violating as many rules as he can, taking curbs, cutting across turf and sidewalks, and running stop signs. He loves laws, but he loves playing with them, too, and this ride is all about play.

As the ride continues, Doug releases reality and enters into a fantasy of the pineal gland, the anatomical third eye that senses light and alters with the seasons. Feeling the power of his engine and of his crazy impulse to annihilation, he dreams of powering his pineal to reach the speed of light and turn into energy itself.

An hour later, far beyond South Shore, in a black neighborhood of tidy yards and well-kept middle class homes, Doug comes back to earth. He decelerates and turns around. By the time they have returned to Woodlawn, and are riding north on Kimbark Street half a mile from the Golden Rectangle, Doug is relaxed and ready for sleep. He is so ready for the ride to end that he is annoyed when the car in front of them slows and stops in the middle of the block, and angry when an oncoming car draws up beside it to block the street.

When the drivers roll down their windows and shout at each other over the R&B music blaring from their speakers, his anger turns to fear. Doug isn't sure what to do. He doesn't want to do anything to attract notice. He decides to wait, but on his left, two young men exit a six-flat, descend the crumbling front stairs, and approach the passenger side of the car on the left to argue with the men in the car. Another group descends from a six-flat on the right to start up the sidewalk in their direction.

When a young man with a big crocheted hat around his Afro slows to stare at Melissa, whom Doug has forgotten and who suddenly feels like dead weight, the hair on his neck stands up.

"What you staring at?" the man demands. He stops. He sways, and curses them.

Doug suddenly feels like an unprepared, unprotected kid of the wrong race in the wrong place. He realizes that the bike could buy a few hits of heroin. He panics. He turns his front wheel left and accelerates at maximum power, which is, unfortunately, far less than fantasy would have it. They pull forward haltingly in slow motion. Fortunately, Melissa puts her weight exactly where he needs it. They roll noisily between two parked cars and onto the sidewalk.

Another group of men materializes directly ahead of them. Doug can't imagine how they got there. He isn't seeing things right. He swerves onto the strip of grass between the sidewalk and street, narrowly missing the men and an open car door. As they begin to speed away, he hears the door slam and a man shouting angrily. Doug regains the street, where they almost fall, and continues to accelerate toward the end of the block. When he hears shouts gathering behind them, he runs the stop sign. Fortunately, the cross street is empty of traffic.

Just as he dares to hope that they are safely away, Melissa shouts, "They're after us! In a car!"

Doug hears a car gaining on them. At the next intersection,

he takes a curb. He gains the grass and then the sidewalk. He is focused on its uneven surface when the car speeds by. His ears register a sound wake of honking and engine tapping, and then the round sound of men's laughter. He halts in consternation. "Shit! Shit. Shit. Shit!"

"I can't believe it. They were laughing at us!" Melissa, too, begins to laugh.

Doug starts slowly, realizing, for the first time, that the boundaries of the university can be seen from two sides. When he rides carefully up the street to the relative safety of the dorm, and stops in the closest driveway, he is still shaking. He tries to control it, but can't, and realizes that in all his years growing up in the south suburbs he never experienced a real threat. The city's violence seemed like a dark game that allured him with transgression, but now his perception of being in charge of his mind, his choices, and his destiny, which he enjoyed an hour ago in the confidence of inexperience, has shattered so suddenly and completely that he may never be able to recover and reunite its jagged fragments.

Melissa slides off her helmet. Tonight, she is the one wearing his signature smirk. "So, is this how you impress your girlfriends?"

"I'm glad it was only you," he returns grumpily. When he has put the bike away, though, and they are walking in silence up the stairs to their rooms, he adds, "Seriously. I'm glad it was you. Most girls would have panicked, and then anything could have happened. Those guys laughed at us, but they could just as easily have killed us." Recovering his edge, he says, "From now on I'm calling you Missy.

"Why?"

"Because you're as poised as a preppie."

4

Jazz

John is standing in the common room of Blackwood Hall watching Doug, who is sitting on the sofa with his feet on the coffee table and his arms spread out on the back of the sofa. He has his mother's car for the weekend and has announced he is thinking of driving north if anyone can come up with a good idea about where to go. Students have gathered around him like iron filings on a magnet, and each is vying to sell Doug on whatever fantasy got them through a tedious week of study in the library. It has been bitterly cold since the beginning of winter quarter and they go out as little as possible—and all have cabin fever.

Doug knows his popularity will wane the minute he makes his decision, so he is lingering over every request. First he is enthusiastic about a *ceilidh* in Bridgeport, then about improv at Second City, then a movie at the Biograph Theater, then John Fahey at the Old Town School of Folk Music, and finally Segovia playing solo at Orchestra Hall. John suspects that Doug will do what he likes best, which is eat out in Greektown, probably at Diana's, and go to a second run movie house to see the Exorcist again. Fortunately for John, his plans do not depend on Doug. John is planning to catch the next Illinois Central train downtown to hear Dizzy Gillespie play.

On his way out, John pauses beside Melissa. "The court jester."

Melissa turns to him and puts her hand on his arm. She pleads, "I'll go stir crazy if I don't get out. Can I come with you?"

John hesitates. Music is his refuge outside of university, and away from his student friends. But Melissa is the one he can count on to see things differently, the one he can talk to about anything. On the other hand, she knows almost nothing about music, and is unlikely to appreciate a jazz genius.

John shrugs vaguely and turns back to Doug in hopes that Melissa will lose interest.

"It's not safe to go alone, you know," she persists.

"You going to protect me?" he asks with a half smile.

"I can scream. And I have a Swiss Army knife."

"Better leave it," he says halfheartedly. "We have to catch the train in twenty minutes."

"I'll get my coat!"

Melissa reappears minutes later covered in layers of army-navy surplus. She is wearing Canadian snow boots, men's wool army pants, a parka with an orange-lined, fur-fringed hood, and a scarf that shows only her bug-eyed glasses. She looks like a three hundred pound Iditarod racer. John is mortified. But as they walk toward the train stop, his knees start to freeze in his jeans. It is the coldest night yet, well below zero, and the beginnings of a blizzard have dusted the sooty piles of ice on the midway.

John pulls down his balaclava and hurries through the arctic night, Melissa beside him, trailing clouds of breath. When he reaches the station platform, he heads for the heat lamps. They stamp and jump and pace until the train arrives, and then they rush on board to find a warm seat. John chooses one from which he can watch Hyde Park fly by.

Melissa sits across from him, unwraps her face, and starts to gossip about the laws of physics, comparing those she likes with those she doesn't. He wants to leave all that behind. He stares out the window and hopes that his disinterest will deter her. It doesn't. When she says she intends to delve deeply into the meaning of Avogadro's number, he smiles.

Melissa looks at him as if he put a cockroach on her dinner plate. "Being smarter doesn't mean you can laugh at me."

"Sorry, but Avogadro's number is just a ratio. It doesn't have any deeper meaning."

Melissa eyes him skeptically and starts talking about electromagnetism and how it explains the way people are fried like bacon when they fall onto the third rail of the El. After a few minutes she stops and stares at him intently. "So what are you thinking about?"

"I'm just trying to relax so I can enjoy the music."

Melissa's face opens as if he is a cat and she accidentally shut his tail in a door. "Of course! This is Friday night, our chance to get out into the real world." She flashes him a dazzling smile, laughs joyfully and adds infectiously, "It's just all so exciting!"

Suddenly John is thinking about electricity and magnetism and wondering how she is able to close some kind of a circuit between them. He forgets about relaxing. He wants to be as excited as she is about everything, and to explore their new connection. Before he knows it, though, the train slows, she rewraps her face, and he begins to think he imagined the hidden side of her that he just glimpsed for the first time.

The next part of the journey is like an urban boot camp. They exit the rail car and run an obstacle course of tunnels, snow-covered sidewalks, slick metal staircases, screeching elevated trains, and transfers that test their transit map-reading skills. When they reach their final stop on the Near North Side, they skate on the sidewalk ice past steam rising from street vents and people trailing smoke signals of breath; the streets are so slick that cars roll slowly through red lights to keep from skidding, and the air is so cold that John and Melissa scurry shoulder to shoulder.

When John spots the Jazz Cellar sign, he points. They run toward it, laughing, and come to a stop, face to face, holding each other up. John can feel Melissa's elbow through her jacket, and notices an unexpected thrill, as if she has closed that circuit again. When she pulls down her scarf and smiles that electric smile, he is truly glad that she is with him.

Melissa steps carefully but quickly down the icy stairs into the warm, dark vestibule of the club, where her glasses fog up. The current between them cuts off when he realizes three things: He is on a date, he is embarrassed to be with a woman wearing army pants and a hunting jacket, and he is ashamed he has no money to pay for her.

"So who's Dizzy Gillespie?"

John looks around in embarrassment before whispering, "A world famous jazz musician."

Before he can panic about being unable to pay for Melissa, she hands a couple of bills to the man at the inner door for her own cover charge. With a barely audible sigh of relief John pays next, and makes his way to an empty table at the front—where he proceeds to studiously ignore Melissa and his unstable feelings. He takes off his wet outerwear and drapes it on the chair, wiggles his warming and burning fingers and toes, and then sits down and stretches his legs until they touch the low platform stage.

John studies the instruments sitting on the edge of the stage and looks around the sophisticated interior, which is filled with slick-looking older black couples. The women are dressed to kill and seem full of feminine wiles. He is suddenly glad to be with a girl who doesn't intimidate him and who looks like she belongs with him.

"How do you know so much about this Dizzy guy?" Melissa asks.

"I play sax, trumpet, a bit of keyboard, bass, and blues harp. Thursdays I go down and jam with Muddy Waters at The Hive. He lets young musicians play with him."

"I had no idea."

"I keep my musical life to myself. Not many students play seriously."

Melissa looks at John skeptically.

He starts rambling. "They usually have better instruments, but not always. See the sax on the stand? It's a Conn, not a very good one. He probably hocked his usual one to buy drugs."

Melissa looks forlorn. "That's horrible!"

"You won't see Dizzy's horn until he carries it out."

The current is flowing between them again, but differently. He seems to feel her emotions, which are so intense and unfamiliar that he can't track the conversation. He keeps talking until she looks happier, and then stops. He has no idea what he said and wishes he were alone. Pulling his chair toward the stage, he pretends to study the instruments intently, and is relieved when the lights go down and the ensemble files in and takes up their positions at the piano, drums and saxophone. Dizzy enters last, counts four, raises his trumpet, and begins. His cheeks puff out in his usual style.

Melissa giggles, and whispers, "Look at his cheeks!"

John wants to slide under the table. Anyone who knows

anything about jazz knows that Dizzy plays that way, and now he's not so sure she belongs with him. Within moments, though, John is lost in the music and the audience. With light and precise applause, and a few remarks, they make it clear that they want the best, and will know it when they hear it. The ensemble draws in their energy, and, as far as John can tell, turns it into improvisations that test the limits of their talent and experience.

After a few standards, and several memorable solos, the saxophonist—an eccentric character in bare feet—begins to pace like a caged cat. He raises his arm to the ceiling and turns his face to the floor. Dizzy and the other musicians frown. After a delay, the saxophonist begins a conventional riff, but just before resolving it, alters it unexpectedly. He continues in this way, spooling out familiar melodies and twisting them at the last minute, teasing the audience with ever-clearer expectations that he never meets— until a wave of laughter spreads through the room and breaks against the walls. At the end of his solo, he plays a long riff and resolves it neatly.

As the audience laughs and applauds, the ensemble exchanges amused smiles: he has surprised them. John glances warily at Melissa and sees that she is laughing. She may not have appreciated that evanescent moment to its fullest, but she got the joke, and liked it. He feels the current flow again. She is heightening his enjoyment of the music. She belongs here with him. Their friendship has reached a new level.

Later, after the end of the second set, when they have exited to shuffle east on Oak Street, John says excitedly, "What about that phrasing! I was surprised the guy on keyboard altered the chord progression with the diminished seventh. And Dizzy's rubato! You know, he was playing with the band the way the sax player did, just in a more sophisticated way."

"I have no idea what you're talking about, but that was the wittiest conversation I've heard since coming to U of C!"

John is surprised and pleased at her interest. When they reach the Illinois Central train again, he sits beside her, leans in close, and speaks into her ear. He tells her about his playing, his record collection, and his musician friends. He explains the subtle form of chord jazz, which enables musicians to compete by creating once in forever improvisations of arresting immediacy, and to reveal the genius of their souls without words.

"I didn't know you could be so passionate, or could open up like this! I always think of you keeping all your thoughts and feelings to yourself," she says.

"Likewise!"

When they return to the dorm, hands numb inside heavy wool mittens, John invites her to come to his room for a cup of tea and to look at his record collection. Later, when they are sitting side by side on his small bed warming their hands on cups of boiling water, John watches the tea bag release amber swirls and allows his thoughts to eddy around the best sets he's heard. He shares their high points with Melissa, who is attentive and quiet.

When he pauses, she sets down her cup, sighs deeply, and takes off her glasses. She leans back against the wall. He pulls up one knee and sits sideways to face her. He feels happy, very happy. Being with her in his room reminds him of sitting at home with his sweet older sister. After a bit, Melissa smiles knowingly and undoes her long hair so that it fans out over her shoulders and falls on a pillow. In this unguarded moment, she becomes soft and feminine and pretty.

John realizes with a start that she has been hiding that part of herself in class and in the library. It worked so perfectly that he could always think clearly. Now his urge to lay down beside her is scattering his thoughts. His mind is filled by an image of reaching out and touching the skin below her ear.

"I'm glad you let me tag along, and that you wore that balaclava! You looked like you could handle anything," she says brightly. "And your company is such a relief. Most guys around here are snooty, or arrogant, or horny, or neurotic, or trapped in some kind of intellectual bubble, and they're not half as bright as you are!"

"Thanks, I guess," he laughs.

"Well, it's true. I'm still not sure I like Alan, but I liked you right away. But that's just normal. Everyone likes you."

"Everyone likes my answers to the homework questions."

"Well, you're at the top of the nerd heap, but you've got horse sense, too. I mean it's hard to find your bearings in a place where everyone has different ideas about right and wrong. You're one of the few who can do it. I can too, but it's hard because I keep getting pulled out of my circle of comfort, which is where I want to be all the time. You know?"

"No."

Melissa looks surprised. "Well, what I mean is, if you think of me as existing as a point within a circle, I like to be at the center, because I like to stay as far as possible from the edge. Doug wants to be inside, but as close to the edge as possible. You know?"

He laughs. "No."

"But what do you think about what I just said?"

"I think you're taking math too seriously."

"Be serious! You're the only person I can talk to about this kind of thing. What do you think about our collective amorality?

I know you've noticed."

"Amorality? I don't know if I'd call it that. We have different personalities and come from different places. But I think you're onto something in Doug's case."

"And Sarah's. Not only has she—well, I don't know if she would want me to say."

"There's a difference right there. She'd never hesitate to gossip."

"Let's just say we have different ideas about sex and drugs and loyalty, but I can respect and care about her, or anyone who follows their own rules. As long as I can tell what they are, and as long as they let me follow mine."

"I think I know what you're trying to say. I have to struggle to respect certain people."

Melissa smiles and takes off her flannel shirt and another layer of reserve. She pushes up the sleeves of her T-shirt and sips her second tea contentedly.

"I hope I haven't done anything to make you feel ..."

"Oh, no! You're different. You, like, have a circle that radiates from deep inside. It's like you don't have to think about what you should do, or push it on other people."

This compliment is personal and idiosyncratic, and therefore intimate. John can feel his face flush. He changes the subject. "Um, you want to hear some Blues?"

They stand together in front of his towering shelves, which he made from cement blocks and wooden planks. "Here are the blues records, classical, jazz, folk, R&B, Latin, and rock."

"I've never seen so many albums in one place! How can you find what you want?"

"I'll show you."

He shows her some favorites and hums the melodies. She

laughs and teases him about his humming. He has never felt so happy. He changes his mind about the music and puts on an old Bossa Nova 78. They listen to its upbeat strains and thumb through his records.

After a while she says in a low voice, "That music you're playing is really getting under my skin. It's so … gosh John, you're amazing! You're not stuck in the Ivory Tower, you know all kinds of people, and you leave the Golden Rectangle without freaking out. I admire how you pass right through the invisible, arbitrary boundaries that hold in the rest of us."

"I don't think people are so easily contained, physically or mentally."

"Maybe, but some are bolder than others. Think of Zeke. He crosses any and all boundaries, but only in his mind, and only because he thinks everyone else is stupid. And Doug leaves his student role physically and mentally, but only as a game, or on a dare. I want to escape the elitism here, which should be easy for a blue-collar girl, but I'm too conformist. And April and Alan crossed barriers to get together, but then turned around and drew a new circle around themselves."

"You make everyone sound trapped."

"We are! All of us are dry-labbing life. Except you, you're out there living it."

Melissa smiles and sits on the floor to examine the bottom shelf of John's records. As she runs her fingers along the albums' edges and titles, he feels as if she is touching him. He kneels behind her and reaches over her shoulder to pull out an album, stopping short when she tips her head and her thick hair falls away to expose her collarbone. As he watches her shoulders move gently with her breath, his eyes caress the curves of her neck and breasts. Without thinking, he presses his lips softly to her hair and whispers, "You're not like everyone else either."

Melissa freezes. He feels uneasy, and then alarmed. She stands, takes her coat, and walks out with one backward look of reproach. When the door closes, John stares at it, stunned, expecting her to return, unable to accept that she has gone without a word.

He feels bereft. Now that the connection is severed, he craves the current that was flowing between them. In fact, he feels sick. He must have caught something. He crawls into bed but cannot sleep. He gives up on rest, gets up and wanders to Doug's room, where a light is still on. John knocks and enters, and begins rambling about how strange he feels. Doug interrupts and says "I got bad news for you, bud. You're love sick."

"What?"

"You're in love. And everybody knows but you and Missy."

"That's ridiculous. I have a cold. Or the flu."

Doug shakes his head. "Nope, you fell. Big time. The good news is she doesn't know. She's been crying on Sarah's shoulder, saying she thought you were different but all you really wanted was to get in her pants."

John blushes, sits hard on the floor and looks at his hands. "That's not true. I just, I felt—"

"You just wanted to get in her pants. That's good. Any guy with a girl in his room at night would feel that way. Which makes it the perfect cover story."

"She stopped talking to me," John says. He feels like crying. He feels like punching the floor. He grunts irritably and says, "Why do I feel like this?" He pulls up his knees, hugs them, and crosses his ankles.

"Let's stick to the subject. The way you smooth it over is

you tell her you got carried away by the music and gave in to an impulse and didn't mean anything by it. You apologize."

"But I didn't do anything wrong."

"That's what you think. That's not what she thinks. If you make it like it was a mistake then things go back the way they were. And it was a mistake."

"If I am in love, shouldn't I face it? Be honest?"

"Only if you want your heart broken. She isn't ready. She may never be ready."

"How will I know when she's ready?"

"Don't worry about it. You'll know."

5

Emergency Room

Sitting in Harper Library looking out the window, Melissa feels the wheel of study grinding away her day. Although her studies are just as compelling as they were before—perhaps even more so—she simply can't concentrate.

The longer, warmer days bypass her focus and speak directly to her body. She feels like a monarch butterfly, ready to fly away to milkweed plants and mud puddles on her way to the breeding place. But she can't. Bound by responsibility, she is years away from breeding. Still, she is learning less every week. She needs a break. And she needs inspiration. She does not want to run away and drop out the way a sophomore in the dorm did last week, but she also does not want to burn out.

Melissa stands, leaves her books and bag on the table, picks up her jacket, and exits to the street. Outside, the trees are still bare but the first of the annuals are in, and the snow has all melted. She has a vague idea of where to find the emergency room, and by following the signs is soon inside. She talks her way past the security guards and goes directly to the reception desk, where she is pleasantly surprised to meet Jerome Beaulieu's girlfriend Livonia. She has met Livonia at the restaurant, and talked with her about her work as a nurse. Melissa tingles with anticipation. The moment is magical. The ER is slow, the staff is bored, and Livonia is sympathetic to Melissa's dreams of becoming a doctor—and to her present burden of sterile bookishness and her itch to know something about the real world of medicine.

"Wait just a moment," Livonia says. She absently touches the afro that frames her heart-shaped face, and then releases her full lips into a luminous smile that softens the formality of her careful poise, dignity, and clear enunciation. "I'll see if Dr. Stein is free."

Livonia disappears through the double swinging doors beside reception. Not long after, a barrel-chested bear of a man with a black beard, who looks unnervingly like Jerry Rubin of the Chicago Seven, bursts through the doors. "Melissa? Come with me."

Melissa follows him with some trepidation, but is soon savoring her first moment of being on the inside of something medical, of taking in the complexity of a space where every square inch is dedicated to saving lives. Cramped and well worn, the emergency suite looks like an old locker room divvied up by curtains and stuffed with stainless steel and plastic technology. It looks like what it is: A century-old hospital that has been kept up-to-date.

Stein is wearing blue jeans and is refreshingly familiar and forthright. "I'm starved for contact with the outside world—and for coffee. Get me a coffee from the cafeteria. You do that for me and I'll see what I can do for you."

"Yes sir," Melissa says with military precision. "But which way is it?"

Stein gestures vaguely toward the rear of the emergency suite, grabs a hanging patient chart, and disappears down the hall on the left behind a curtain. Melissa checks her pockets for money, and is relieved to find a few dollars in change that she had been planning to use for laundry. She spots a sign that says "cafeteria" and follows it out of the suite and down to the basement. There are no more signs. Melissa has no idea where to go next. She feels as if she has failed Stein's admissions test. She has never been in a large complex of interconnected buildings, and soon gets lost in the labyrinthine utility corridors. She discovers a cryptic system of color-coded stripes of floor tape that seem to parallel the gray-painted pipes suspended from the ceiling. Finally, she stops a friendly-looking nurse in a crisp white hat and asks for directions. Half an hour later, she returns to the Emergency Room carrying a paper cup full of lukewarm, gray-brown, machine-made coffee.

Dr. Stein takes the coffee, sets it on a ledge, and pulls her into a curtained alcove to let the patient, a young man with a dislocated shoulder, squeeze her hand as a distraction while Stein pulls the arm into place. Then he winks and pulls her into the next alcove to see an older woman who is groaning and holding her belly, but who is incongruously dressed up in a thick gray wig and elaborate makeup. Using Melissa as a foil, Stein explains that the woman's mysterious set of complaints would guarantee admission to the hospital if she were sore across her lower ribs. The woman immediately develops that symptom. Stein gives Melissa a look of significance and retreats into a closet-like office to close the door and explain that the patient is trying to sneak into the hospital for some reason, perhaps to get food or because she has been evicted. He "broke her story" to keep hospital beds open for any real emergencies that come in.

A few minutes later, while Melissa is still reeling from the revelation that Stein is more like a sheriff in a western than a doctor in a soap opera, Stein sends her to help a nurse with a patient named Mr. Jackson. Melissa is happy to see that the nurse is Livonia, but alarmed to see that Mr. Jackson is lying on a gurney—a wheeled, cushioned stretcher—thrashing wildly as he tries to pee over its side rail. When Livonia stops him, he winds up to take a swing at her. Her hands are on the intravenous line, so Melissa dashes forward and reaches for Mr. Jackson's arm in time to block his right hook, and to sniff the source of his belligerence. Fortunately, he is so drunk and feeble that she can hold him easily while Livonia binds his IV and then his arms to the gurney with long, soft strips of gauze. Mr. Jackson relents, fills a urinal, and passes out. Livonia hangs the urinal on the gurney and caps it, and asks Melissa to stay with Mr. Jackson until the upstairs staff receive the formal nursing report.

Melissa waits, bemused. An hour ago, she wouldn't have believed that the delivery of medical care might entail force and guile. She has seen drunks lash out, but it never occurred to her that they would do that in a clinic. She must have assumed that everyone would put on their best underwear and wait patiently to take a turn with the doctor. Now she can see that derelicts are brought in against their will, and that polite people may risk needles and drugs to get a night in the hospital.

When Livonia returns, she takes time to explain that Mr. Jackson received a panhandling windfall that he used to buy enough hard liquor to push his alcohol level into the lethal range. The staff usually dries him out in the emergency room and sends him on his way, but now he will have to stay in an inpatient ward until he is out of danger. Melissa is amazed and disturbed when Livonia looks wistfully at Mr. Jackson and says, without crosstalking, "One time, he was fine. Now he's using T's and B's, and drinking antifreeze."

Livonia shows Melissa the penny-like scars on Mr. Jackson's legs that show where he injected pentazocine and tripelennamine, and the bulging belly caused by his alcoholic liver failure. Before she can continue this education, an alarm rings and red lights flash high on the wall above. She runs, and Melissa follows. They reach a room with double doors that resembles an operating suite. Stein, Livonia, and another nurse enter and busy themselves with white and red supply carts. Melissa finds an empty space along the wall and stands still. Stein looks at her and says, "The police found a woman unconscious. No pulse. No telling how long."

Livonia shakes her head. "Should be going to the morgue."

A cart bursts in pushed by two paramedics in blue uniforms. The nurses rip off the patient's clothes and push a tube down her throat as Dr. Stein sticks a line in her neck. On his command, the nurses give injections and then he puts paddles to her chest and shocks her. After several minutes, Stein puts one knee on the gurney and pushes rhythmically on her chest. At first Melissa is carried off by the aggressive excitement in the room, but gradually feels confused and distressed. They are all frustrated at the woman for failing to awaken, at themselves for failing to wake her, and at the situation for forcing them to act in a way they believe to be wrong.

After twenty minutes, Stein snaps, "I'm calling the code. She would have been a vegetable anyway." He drops the paddles and stalks away.

The nurses immediately turn off the equipment and leave, and Melissa is alone with death for the first time. Huge bruises discolor the dead woman's withered breasts and limbs. Her rib cage reminds Melissa of a smashed pumpkin. She looks to have died in a vicious assault. Melissa has never seen such violence. The shooting at Beaulieu's was quiet and quick, and hidden. This code was like a battle in a war against death that medicine wages systematically and—at least at times—unwisely and ineffectively.

She has known that doctors often intervene well after the damage is done, but she has never before felt it, or recognized that in doing too little too late, society wastes resources and runs on rage and sorrow. Melissa is shocked and confused, very confused, about what doctors do. She hopes they do more than battle death, offer costly breaks from self-destruction and criminality, and act as if life matters only when it is about to end. She cannot tear herself away from the corpse that has been violated. She wants to do something—anything—to honor the dead. After looking about helplessly, she throws a gown over the body and exits quietly. When she emerges, Dr. Stein is writing on a chart.

"You okay?"

Melissa feels that her mettle is being tested, and that she will pass if she acts as if everything is all right. "I'm fine. Thank you for letting me learn something real."

"Transport should have taken Jackson upstairs an hour ago."

Melissa notices that Stein is doing his best to look brave and confident even though he is still very upset, and realizes with surprise that they have bonded in some way. "I'll do it. Thank you for everything."

Dr. Stein pats Melissa's arm collegially and hands her Mr. Jackson's paper chart to take to the resident on the fifth floor. Stein points to the elevator and gives her a few instructions before disappearing into a curtained alcove. She grabs the gurney and wrestles it for a few moments before realizing she must unlock the brake. Then she pushes it awkwardly down the narrow hall, taking comfort from doing a simple task that has a clear and sensible goal.

"You can't take him," declares an angry voice.

Melissa looks up to see a rangy black man in a green shower

cap waving a pink piece of paper.

Livonia appears. "Val Beaulieu, if you don't take him, we going to do it!"

Val and Livonia begin to argue. Melissa slowly gathers that Val is Jerome's brother and an employee in the transportation department, and that he is refusing to take Mr. Jackson upstairs because the triplicate requisition form specifies a wheelchair whereas Mr. Jackson is now on a gurney, and union rules require a new requisition. Livonia sent it in an hour ago, but it has not gone through the system, and the patient's condition and the crowding of the Emergency Room require immediate action.

Melissa doesn't want to break the rules, but she wouldn't put rules before patients, so when Val heads to the reception desk to call his supervisor, she makes a break for the elevator. Val relents. He helps push Mr. Jackson's cart inside. She is amused until the door closes behind them and she realizes that she is in way over her head. For one thing, she recognizes him from the night of the shooting. Secondly, though he seemed to be a stickler for rules, he shakes Mr. Jackson awake and mutters an offer of illegal drugs. Jackson is too drunk to reply. When the door opens, Val gestures for Melissa to go straight down the hall. She is reluctant to leave the patient alone with Val, but knows nothing of the hospital and feels powerless to contradict him. She decides to walk backward and pull the cart while Val pushes it.

They soon pass a sign that reads "General Medicine Ward," and then a desk behind which the top of a woman's head bobs, and a series of inpatient rooms. When they stop at number 503, Melissa hears a hostile voice demand, "What are you doing?"

She turns to sees a man standing with his arms crossed whose steely face—all planes and angles—is outlined by an elaborately trimmed beard. He is wearing white painter's pants with a buttoned-down shirt and a tie. The name on his badge is Dr. Polter.

Val's face shows no emotion. "Mr. Jackson for room 503."

"You can't put that dirtball in the same room with the Provost of the University!"

Melissa is shocked, first by the feeling that the small world of Hyde Park comes together here in the hospital, and second by the—to her—unthinkable presumptuous arrogance of Polter. She feels a flash of embarrassment at wanting to be his colleague, and a moment of recognition that Mr. Jackson practically lives here. She is glad that no one recognizes her, and that she is not yet part of this world. She is not ready to be.

"What he say?" Mr. Jackson asks Val, his face suddenly alert.

Val's eyes narrow. Melissa feels a chill, and senses that Val might be dangerous. Val pulls the cart in the door behind him and Melissa pushes it until it is next to the far bed of the semi-private room.

In the near bed a man with silver hair, whose gown is splotched with blood, says resignedly, "Please, don't be concerned Dr. Polter. I'm sure you have other patients to attend to."

Mr. Jackson squints at Polter. "You that doctor took care of me last time?"

"Yes I am, and you are not the kind of patient who should stay in this room."

Mr. Jackson raises himself on one elbow and puts a scarred leg over the edge of the gurney. As he tries to stand, he lets out a stream of abuse—every third word of which is "motherfucker"—at which point Dr. Polter turns red, and the Provost, who is already pale, turns the color of lye-soaked codfish.

Val suddenly cries out "Mr. Jackson!" The inebriated man

is reaching down toward a bag on the bottom shelf of the cart. Although his balance is precarious, he jerks up holding a gun in his right hand, and raises it unsteadily in the direction of Dr. Polter. Melissa watches stupefied as Jackson sways, and tries to take aim. He lurches left, drops his right arm, and pulls the trigger. Val and Polter move to take the gun, but Mr. Jackson has already aimed and fired again.

The Provost flies out of the room like a sprinter at a high school track meet, IV line flapping behind him, wispy hair bouncing with his stride as a tiny nurse zips past, shouting something in Filipino. But when Melissa looks back at Mr. Jackson, the gun is gone, Mr. Jackson is out cold in bed, and Val is already pushing the gurney toward the elevator.

Melissa leaves in the direction of the Provost. She finds the staircase and takes the exit. Although they are in the Golden Rectangle in a secure facility, there is nothing truly safe here. While the sacredness of life and the possibility of saving it are palpable—in the love and care of the staff, and in the suffering they ease—the care is at times gentle and generous, and at other times violent and punitive. It is a microcosm of the Great Society that is forming, and of which she and her cohort will become a part as they step up and take charge of its simmering potential for good.

6

On Belay

The endless study of disembodied artifacts of thought is making John feel like an archaeologist. His world is becoming a stone tomb, and he is beginning to think like Doug, who says that the dead—scholars in this case—rob sleep from the living. When John spots a posted announcement of the Outing Club's upcoming spring climbing trip, he imagines that he is standing in the North Woods, and resolves to join the club and to get out of the city.

At the Thursday evening organizational meeting, a graduate student named Grady describes the upcoming trip: Club members will meet at his office in the basement of the Quadrangle at 7:00 a.m. on Saturday, drive five hours to Devil's Lake, Wisconsin, practice technical rock climbing for several hours in the afternoon, and drive back that evening. Grady shows off the club's new Perlon ropes, explains the club's policies about the sharing of expenses, and invites those present to sign up.

John signs up first. An enthusiastic Grady leads him and several other new members to the club lockers and shows them its precious cache of old climbing and camping gear. John learns that Grady's a graduate student in particle physics who sometimes participates in experiments at Fermilab, and who usually works the midnight to 8:00 a.m. shift on the electromagnet in the basement of the quadrangle. He is small and wiry, has a bony frame, and wears black glasses and a carabiner on his wrist.

On Saturday morning, when Grady shows up in a dented old Rambler station wagon with a rusted bottom, John takes the passenger seat and two women hop in the back. One, a laconic woman of unknown age and affiliation, has long blonde hair and wears aviator glasses with clothes from the army-navy store. The other is a nervous undergraduate who takes a great interest in John's grades and seems to view him as a potential competitor. Because of their mutual interest in climbing, the ill-suited and rough-edged group is soon getting along smoothly.

As they roll by the familiar prairie with its black fields, large dairy barns, and clumps of trees, he feels expansive, and thrills to the bucolic terrain he once took for granted. Within the hour they have left behind the human quagmire in Hyde Park and been soothed by the monotony of the highway and the seeming constancy of heartland farms.

Devil's Lake is not far from where John grew up, and yet he has never seen it. When they reach its car park, he sees a sparse forest with lichen-covered breakdown and a floor of trails interrupted by stairs of rough black stone built by the Civilian Conservation Corps during the Great Depression. They find the lake in a quarry-like black bowl where they stop to watch a free climber with gray hair scale a rock face with indentations and cracks that offer hand and toe-holds that climbers have mapped into an astonishing number of routes.

The taciturn trip leader, Grady, is soon dangling from a rope on a popular climbing route called Easy Overhang. The other end of the rope loops up around a tree trunk and down around the waist of a belayer standing with the crowd of beginners at the bottom of the popular forty-foot cliff. After scrambling up the pockmarked rock Grady raises a power fist, then rappels to the bottom in a few long bounces. He lands on his keester, jumps to his feet, and turns to face the group with a smile. "John?"

Wondering why Grady picked him, John approaches slowly, and ties the rope around his waist with a bowline knot. As Grady wraps the other end of the rope around his own waist, he reviews the verbal commands climbers use to communicate, then steps back. John moves up to the rock and takes hold of the slight outcroppings he saw Grady use for finger and palm holds, feeling the weight of the coarse, bulky rope hang over his sagging leather belt. His shout ricochets off the rock: "On belay!"

From then on, John is aware of nothing but hard, cold rock and the rhythm and balance of his body. As the spatial pattern of his moves and contrapuntal rising of the rope fall into a rhythm, John thinks of listening to the piano player and drummer before improvising a riff on his sax. He crawls smoothly upward like a lizard until he gets stuck below a big bulge in the cliff. Unable to feel the handhold above, he presses his sneaker against a tiny ridge with his toes until his left foot weakens and jerks up and down in what Grady calls sewing machine knee. Finally, taking the risk of heaving his body up with his right foot and left palm, John's right fingertips find a tiny ledge above the bulge that he can use to leverage his weight.

John resumes his rhythm. In a few short minutes, he is standing at the top of the bluff above Devil's Lake feeling light and free. Grady beams up like a gambler who has bet on the right horse. John smiles back. He guesses that Grady chose a beginner he thought would persevere and set the example of enjoying the challenge. John undoes the bowline and bounds down a dusty gray trail at the back, laughing to find he could have easily reached the top by walking.

While Grady belays the next beginner, he shows John the path of the rope that goes from the climber's bowline up over the top of the cliff, down around the belayer's back, and out into his hand. He then teaches John how to lean back and pull the rope taut to arrest a fall, and how to keep tension on the rope without interfering with the climber's independence.

When the climber is halfway to the top Grady shouts to her to take a fall. She looks back nervously. John watches her uncomfortably. It is all too easy to imagine what will happen if she falls. When she lets go, though, Grady leans back and catches her easily. She regains her hold on the rock and continues upward.

The next thing John knows, Grady is tying a bowline around his own waist and wrapping the other end around John. After doing a final check of the rig, and of John's understanding, Grady begins to climb. When he is halfway up, he looks back at John and then jumps. To John's surprise, he feels no fear; his body leans confidently back, his left hand acts instinctively, and the rope twangs taut with Grady dangling like a scarecrow at the other end.

John is overtaken by a strange logic. He can't fail because the consequences are unacceptable. He's reliable because that's what the situation demands. He can depend on himself, and others can depend on him. No classroom experience has taught him as much, and no subject has captured his fancy like this. John loves the geometry of climbing, its intimacy with the earth's substance, and, most surprisingly, the feeling of being joined to and responsible for another. He has a strange déjà vu and feels as if he has always been a climber, but has only just found out.

On the drive home, while they are eating dinner at a truck

stop, Grady begins a conversation that seals a change in John's life. "I pick the first climber carefully. If he climbs easily, no one will freeze or whine. The least likely to succeed goes last."

Grady turns to a girl he chose to go last and says, "You did great, though. You went straight to the top without a hitch. Or a half hitch. Ha!"

She replies in a lower East Side accent, "I'm a dancer, so it feels natural. I'd like to do it again."

"You want to climb a mountain? Be with guys when they wipe their noses on their hands, and fart a lot, and take a leak behind you on a narrow rock ledge?"

"Depends on the guys. Some guys know how to behave. Today was nice."

"John here's my man. You can take a leak on a ledge, can't you John?"

John doesn't reply. Grady may be a brilliant graduate student in experimental physics, but his behavior in mixed company is lacking.

"What are you doing this summer?" Grady asks, pulling a tiny calendar book out of his shirt pocket.

John replies, "I don't know yet."

"Need a job?"

"Yeah. I've got to make around fifteen hundred."

"I can get you a job at a cannery near Juneau. Hard work, good money."

John is getting used to Grady's blunt delivery and single-mindedness, but is not sure whether he is unbelievably decisive or attempting a joke. "Are you serious? That would be really cool."

"You said it. You'll freeze your ass. Ha! We can share gas and driving, leave after finals and kayak Glacier Bay. On the way back, we'll climb the Rockies, if you get in shape. You have to do one-handed and fingertip pull-ups. You can work out with me at Bartlett every morning. I start at 7:00 p.m. Ha!"

John is stunned to be offered this opportunity that he didn't know existed and yet is exactly what he wants, but is able to reply without hesitation. "Count me in."

7

Lascivious Costume Ball

On the night of April 29, Doug steps out of the vestibule of Blackwood Hall into chilly evening air. He is on his way to the Lascivious Costume Ball, one of the main events of the annual Walpurgisnacht Festival. Doug thinks it's the perfect University of Chicago party because pasty intellectuals with a sense of humor use Goethe's allusions to pagan rituals as a ploy to get laid, or at least to flash and be flashed.

The last snow had melted over a month ago, leaving layers of freeze-dried dog excrement lying in bare heaps on the frozen ground. Doug picks his way carefully along the sidewalk, his bare feet painfully cold against the grainy concrete. His trench coat barely keeps him warm enough, but he is determined to wear nothing else. He wants to get into the for ball free, and the only way to do that is to arrive at the door naked. Although the warmest and safest way to do that is to wear a coat and then flash the guard at the door, he doesn't like to "cheat" that way—and certainly doesn't want any of the women to do that.

What he really wants is to walk in, drop his trench coat, and draw the attention and accolades of all the women present by displaying his manly physique and well-hung family jewels. He tells himself that if he gets into the mood he'll do just that: boldly drop the trench coat and enjoy the blessings of Naturism.

As Doug walks toward the quadrangle, however, he holds his coat more and more tightly around him. At the corner of 59th Street, he almost backs out. He seriously considers going back to get his underwear, in which he can still be admitted to the ball for half price, but decides against it. To keep warm, he walks briskly along the Midway. Protected by the dark and preoccupied by the cold, he forgets the prospect of nudity until he rounds the corner of the quadrangle and sees the entrance to the designated classroom building. With its gargoyles, bright lights, and blackboards, it seems to be the worst possible place to take off his clothes.

Fortunately, his entry to the ball is easy. A group of ten men stands clustered at the entrance, hoping to see a nude woman. In their company, Doug feels completely at ease as a flasher. Once inside, he goes directly past a cluster of other undergraduate men in trench coats and on to a plastic-bag-lined garbage can labeled "SVNA punch."

"What's SVNA punch?" Doug asks an unshaven student who, clad in boxers, shoes, and a tie, seems to be in charge.

"SVNA stands for Students for Violent Non-Action."

"But what's in it?"

"Kool-Aid and ethanol."

"Ethanol?"

"Yeah. Don't worry; it's pure. It's lifted from the research labs over in Cummings."

"Kool-Aid?"

"Look, you want to get drunk or not?"

"I want to get drunk."

"One SVNA punch coming right up."

The student in charge hands him a small Styrofoam cup. Doug uses a ladle on a string to scoop out a serving for himself that goes down like fire. Looking up at the student, he asks again, "Kool-Aid?"

"Yeah, but we didn't add the water this time." The student smiles wickedly.

Doug admires the efficiency of the beverage. He looks around and makes a quick circuit through the series of linked rooms to see what he can see. He finds a subdued atmosphere with a distinct absence of Bacchanalian revelry. Most of the partiers are pale, asthenic undergraduate men who are fully clothed or wearing trench coats. There are a few women, most of them fully clothed. Doug takes in the scene and concludes that most of the men hoping for a glimpse of a female body will leave seriously depressed. He decides to have another punch, and then another before going on another circuit.

A while later, he is not sure how long, he stumbles into a classroom and spots a pair of breasts facing a group of men in a corner. The woman is wearing a mask and an Elvira wig, but her posture and erect nipples tell him that she enjoys showing off her gorgeous body. There is a constant stream of traffic past her corner as word spreads and every straight man at the party tries to get a look; some discreetly, but most not. Doug can't seem to break into the traffic to get a frontal view.

When he finally pushes awkwardly to the front, he lets go of his unbuttoned trench coat.

"Nice pair," he says when he meets the breasts. "Can I take you home with me?"

"Just the breasts?" she asks.

The voice is familiar. Even now, in his sense-obliterated

65

state, he recognizes the voice as Sarah's, and remembers that he has wanted to see her breasts since orientation day. He staggers, spreads his feet wide to brace himself, and stares dumbly. Slowly, he smiles. Finally he has something to tell his high school friends who brag about their party schools, and about coeds who just want to have a little fun—and don't want to talk about feelings or give men their phone number or demand equal sexual gratification.

Most of the women Doug has met want all those things and more. They are a lot of work and they have their pick of men. The competition is fierce, and he seems always to be losing something he only half-heartedly wants. It has been weeks, maybe months, since he's seen a breast. Now, he will stare and stare and stare and forget all of that. He doesn't notice that his trench coat is sliding down his shoulders. He only notices that his black mood is lifting.

"Nice rod," says Sarah's voice. "You're rising to the occasion."

As Doug smiles his pleasure, there is a flash of light and the sound of a camera shutter. He looks up, startled but stuporous. A fully clothed woman smiles playfully at him. "Just getting a shot for the Daily Maroon campus newspaper."

When she disappears, he grasps what she said, looks down in consternation, and suddenly gets why men wear trench coats to the ball. It is not just to keep warm. He tries to cover his erection with his hand, and then his cup, but it doesn't work. It is so big and stiff that his punch cup hides very little.

The breasts come toward him. An arm takes his. He is vaguely aware of being immersed in nervous laughter as students move away from the photographer.

Everything but the breasts seems distant and unreal. He follows them outside, where they disappear under a sweater.

The cold air braces him. He feels sick and barfs in the bushes. The next thing he knows, he is lying on his bed in the dorm with Sarah, who is naked. As he reaches for her breasts, his erection returns and he slides into oblivion.

8

Cherry

The Friday after the Lascivious Costume Ball, April sleeps in Alan's bed for the first time. The two have been close since fall quarter, an item since winter quarter, and inseparable for weeks now. His balls are blue, he tells her, and he can't bear to be with her any more if she won't sleep with him. They are each committed to distinct and incompatible religions, roots, and families, and that troubles them deeply, but the fundamental problem is that he wants free sex without responsibility while she wants an all-inclusive lifelong union. She relents first. She would rather lose her virginity than lose him, and agrees to sleep with him—just sleep, at first, and he agrees that they needn't go all the way.

That evening, as usual, they eat dinner and study together at the library. And, as usual, Alan can't concentrate on his studies. Everything reminds him of sex: The attraction between negative and positive ions, the taxonomy of dioecious plants, the nude wrestling matches of ancient Sparta, the replication of DNA.

When they finally get back to his room, Alan sits down on the bed to take off his shoes while April, feeling tense, sits down at the table and opens a book.

"Why don't you go to sleep, Alan, I'm going to study for a while."

He doesn't want to be pushy but he is losing patience.

"I thought we'd talked this over."

"Yes, but I just want to go over a few things. I always do this when I have an exam."

"April, the exam is open book and you've studied for it all week and it's not until next week. You have to relax and get some sleep. Besides, it's Shabbos now. The day of rest."

"I'm okay."

He takes off his shoes, his socks, and then his shirt. April glares at him, her heart pounding. She has never seen him without his shirt. His body is both frightening and attractive. As he takes off his pants, she wants to look away but can't. His long, slender legs are covered with black hair which grows as dense as steel wool close to his crotch. The silhouette of his partially erect penis terrifies her. She has not seen a penis since the age of six, when she peeked at her brother through the keyhole in the bathroom door. It seems to her odd and unseemly. As he starts to remove his briefs, she puts her hands over her face.

"No, stop. We agreed on underwear."

He stops, accepting that it will be too much for her, and that the sight of his penis might make her less rather than more aroused. This gives him an idea.

"Do you want me to turn out the lights?"

"Yes," she replies in a small, terrified voice that at first angers him, and then unlocks his kindness—and makes him feel manly and dominant. He walks past her to the door and flips the light switch. She is now between him and the bed. He walks to her chair, puts his hand under her elbow, and draws her gently to her feet. He kisses her, as he has so often.

April feels that he has never kissed her so intensely. Her nervousness shifts: she feels a new sensation between her legs, an ache, which might be pleasurable or uncomfortable. She lets herself go a little bit. Her breathing comes more rapidly. Alan senses her arousal. He has waited for this moment for months. He forces himself to let her make the next move, even though his penis is painfully erect. After a minute she takes off her shirt, shoes, and socks, and finally her pants. He lies down on the bed and she joins him.

The streetlight shines in around the edge of the window shade, illuminating his rock star idols and April's closed eyes. He kisses her and tentatively touches her breast, surprised and excited by the firm but gel-like feel of it. He hopes that she will touch his penis, and then that she won't. He doesn't want to come before she is ready.

April feels exposed and unprotected as fear rises and overwhelms her arousal. Alan reaches behind her, slowly running his hand down her back then pulling her knee over his hip. As his fingers brush against her inner thigh, she draws a sharp breath. Her labia are swelling. She has never felt this. It is fascinating, exciting, and compelling. He brings his hand between her legs and strokes her vulva gently. She does not know what to expect, or how to make sense of what she feels, but doesn't want to stop.

She opens her eyes, stares intensely at Alan, and wonders how she could have thought that she knew him before. Alan interprets this as a sign that she is feeling bolder. He embraces her tightly, pulls her forward and presses his penis against her. The sudden and unexpected feel of Alan's rock-hard penis fills her with revulsion. She turns on her back and clutches the covers.

"Too fast?" he asks solicitously, surprised to feel the thrill of his power over her overcome by a tender urge to protect her—even from himself. He kisses her cheek and waits for her to relax. He waits to feel her desire for him. He has never felt as fulfilled as a man. He knows now what it means to be a lover, and he wants to be hers, her one and only.

"I'm sorry," she says, "I didn't know it would be so hard."

"It'll get easier, until we don't want to stop."

"No, I mean your, your ..."

"My schlong?"

"Yes. I didn't know it got like that."

He is momentarily disoriented. He can't believe how little she seems to know.

"Are you saying you didn't know what an erection was like?"

"I guess so." She turns toward him again. "I want to be close to you Alan. I know what you want now and I want it too. Please be patient. I want to ... go all the way."

He puts his arms around her. She rests her head on his shoulder. They lay quietly for several minutes, adjusting to their new level of intimacy as the eerie screaming of tomcats reverberates in the alley under the window, and a siren speeds toward them before fading away.

April enjoys the sweet warmth of lying together, and the relief of having decided, finally, to give herself to him. She allows herself to anticipate sharing the ultimate intimacy. "I think I love you Alan," she says quietly.

It is Alan's turn to recoil in fear. He remembers his father warning him: "Be careful playing around with girls, son. They fall in love with you, and then they want to get married and have children and bang, your career is over." He remembers his plan to sleep with a blonde, a brunette, and a redhead, maybe all at the same time. He remembers his determination to meet and love and marry a Jewish woman. He remembers his mother's warning: "Don't let some *shiksa* make you forget who you are. You bring me home a nice Jewish girl." He knows that if April brought home a Jewish man it would be over her parents' most strenuous objections. How could they marry? But wasn't that where this was heading?

But how can he stop now? It is too late. He is impossibly entangled and has no one but himself to blame for pushing April so far. Alan realizes clearly and for the first time that he has no idea what he is doing. An hour ago he felt experienced, sophisticated; now, he realizes that he is walking a wire without a net.

April surprised him with her sudden courage. He has to meet her half way. He takes a deep breath and says, "I think I love you too."

9

Finals

F inals week fizzles slowly for Melissa. By the time she finishes
her last exam, all of her friends who will be leaving for the
summer have gone, except John. She helps him pack and then
walks him to the Illinois Central train station on the Midway
where he will begin his long journey west. When he turns back
to wave goodbye, his eyes on fire with enthusiasm, hers prickle
with tears. She stares after him, feeling alone and forlorn, aching
for something she can't name.

She can name the fact that to gain knowledge is to lose
connection with those who don't, which is one reason she is glad
Doug found them an apartment to share this summer where
April, Alan, and Zeke plan to join them in the fall. Doug's father
co-signed the lease, and will be taking them out to dinner tonight
at the Perroquet, a French restaurant in the Loop. Fortunately,
she has a dress, and a hope of blending in.

Walking back along the Midway toward the campus, the
moderate heat and humidity of June dampening her T-shirt and
cut-off jeans, she notices how quiet the birds are that usually
sing in the row of stately elms that lines the sidewalk. Perhaps
they, too, have gone. As she passes Blackwood Avenue, she looks
north to catch a glimpse of the site of the dorm life that was hers
only yesterday, and wonders if sharing an apartment with a small

group of chosen friends next term will be freeing yet filled with intimacy, or forced and fractious. At Kenwood, she turns north to visit Sarah in her new sharehouse. Having felt unmoored as finals approached, they made a blood-sister pinky swear pact to to meet weekly for tea and mutual support.

Sarah, the more venturesome of the two, had moved with Anne into a communal house of Eastern urbanite upperclassmen whom they met only once when applying for their rooms. Melissa is intimidated by Sarah's housemates—who are said to be articulate and sophisticated; she is also curious, feeling pushed by loss, and pulled by life to meet new people who will challenge her to mature.

Melissa slows to enjoy the deep morning shade of the old trees that line Kenwood. After crossing 57th, and then 56th Street, she stops in front of the house. Anne bursts out just then, rolling her eyes wordlessly before stalking up the street toward 55th. Melissa wonders what is going on inside, and feels an urge to ask until she recalls that she can rarely make sense of what Anne is thinking or doing, and that Anne is easily upset.

Melissa pauses to examine the house. She has never entered a single-family home in this neighborhood, and this one seems monumental in comparison to the upstairs apartment in the two-story clapboard home where she grew up.

This yard, like others in the city, is simple. The grass is lush and four or five inches long, signaling neglect. The rough cement walk is fractured, the stairs are tilted, and the paint on the window trim and porch siding is scratched and cracked. These seedy features make it appear comfortable and unpretentious, which offsets the imposing limestone foundation, the three stories of ivy-covered stucco and stone, the peaked slate roof, and the widespread eaves.

Melissa ascends the stairs cautiously, knocks on the dark, heavy wood door, and waits. When no one answers, she enters and finds a room with hooks on the walls and shoes stacked carelessly beneath them. She continues through an inner door of glass panes and pauses on a vermilion bordered Persian rug.

"Who are you?" a male voice demands sharply.

"I'm looking for Sarah?"

"In here. We're having a house meeting," Sarah calls out. "Come on in. Greg is just finishing."

Sarah is sitting on a couch, smiling and patting the cushion beside her. Melissa scoots in, sits quietly, and then notices that Greg is glaring at them. He was likely not intending to finish. Of the ten residents, only two other meek-looking underclass women are present.

Greg is tall and has narrow slouching shoulders, a frizzy dark ponytail, and bird-like features set in a disapproving expression with downturned mouth and wrinkled forehead.

"As I was saying," he says, as if speaking to a bad little brother, "people have to sign up to do the dishes. They're not getting done and they stink."

As Greg goes on in this way for a couple of minutes, Melissa takes note of the room. Sarah's croton and wandering Jew—along with a ficus and schefflera—soften the cushionless window seat; two rickety chairs with presswood patterns and a framed sketch of the Columbia Exposition nod to local history, and a stack of heavy floor pillows suggests that the room may fill with students for parties or more serious gatherings. The house and furnishings are far grander than those of her parents, and homier too. It is a shame that Greg is so very unpleasant. Other student houses must be doing better on the social side—at least she hopes they are.

"Everyone here but you does dishes. *You* should do them instead of talking about it. Sign-up sheet is on the fridge," Sarah says curtly, standing and motioning for Melissa to follow as she heads toward the carpeted, creaking stairway opposite the entry and goes up one flight and into a large room overlooking a cramped backyard with a tall fence. The walls are covered with posters that protest social injustice and are arranged with a good eye for color and shape. Melissa is surprised to see twin beds in opposite corners, Sarah has put her familiar bed spread on the one next to a tall dresser with skewed drawers and a metal government surplus desk with a caned chair. Beside the other bed, which is unmade, is a wide closet overflowing with unpacked boxes that are visible behind a sheer curtain.

"That's Sheryl's bed. She just cleaned up. I kid you not."

Melissa giggles and hops up on the bed. "I didn't know you were sharing a room."

"New members share," Sarah replies. "Tea?"

"Let's."

As Sarah turns on the hotpot on top of the dresser next to the radio, Melissa asks conspiratorially, "Will he retaliate?"

"Greg? Probably. He's touchy. But I'll win. I'll get everyone to walk out next time he runs a meeting that goes into overtime. Maybe I'll call him Pope Greg."

"Is he always so awful?"

"He isn't, really. He's just a large beagle, like my dad. I tried objecting—that works with Dad, but Greg always overrules me. I'll tame him in the end. He'll figure out that I'm the better organizer and realize that he'd rather be arguing with the university than with us."

Melissa giggles. "I'm glad I don't live here. He'd wear me out."

They chat, tell stories, and cheer each other up until they get to the subject of summer jobs, which rouses feelings of trepidation and anticipation.

"What will you do at N.O.R. ... ?"

"NORC. National Opinion Research Center. Same thing as before," Sarah answers.

"Remind me?"

"We do survey research by telephone. I took the call training in the spring, and worked enough hours to get used to it and then get good at it. If all goes well I'll train and monitor beginners."

"Monitor?"

"Calls are monitored to make sure you know how to keep people on the line. They absolutely loathe missing data. They act like it's the end of the world when someone hangs up on you. How about you? Have you uh ... started?"

"It upsets you? Me working in a dog lab?"

"I wouldn't do it."

"The dogs all come from the pound. When they're about to be put down. They would die anyway."

"You're going to have to kill dogs. That's what they do."

"Lucky for me I never had a dog as a pet. When I think of dogs I think of guard dogs that want to bite me. But I take your point. I'm not looking forward to that. I'm looking forward to helping my prof study lung disease. You know how many people die of it? Think of it—suffocating to death because you can't take a breath. And I think it's better to do the research on a dog than on a human. And to respect the dog by making his death a part of a larger purpose."

"Will you ask the dog if he wants to be sacrificed? Or killed?"

"Would you?"

"I'm a cat person. I'd ask a cat and she'd be on your side."

Melissa laughs half-heartedly. "I'm lucky to have the work. If my aunt hadn't worked in the lab I'd be back in Peoria working an assembly line making first aid kits for the soldiers in Vietnam."

Sarah sighs. "That's not fair. It shouldn't be like that."

"It would be nice to be able to do something you think is right and good. We can work for that."

"Change the system from the inside?"

"I hope so."

"Me too. Here's to trying." Sarah goes to the hot pot, puts out the two cups with once-used tea bags, and pours the boiling water. They clink a wordless toast, carefully set the cups on the floor, and sit down on either side of them. As the tea brews and cools, they talk about Alan's summer independent study in a biochemistry lab, which they think will suit his fastidiousness; about April's work as a clerk at Frank Lloyd Wright's Robie house, which now houses university offices and has a small gift shop devoted to his architecture; Zeke's surprising choice to study fine art across the Midway in the studio where the new, small colored windows in Rockefeller chapel had been designed and made; and about Thomas' job working for his father, doing whatever it is that he does.

"Greg is a friend of Thomas," Sarah says, crossing the room to close the door.

"Does Greg supply Thomas with drugs, or does he supply Greg?"

"I'm guessing they both buy from the same source. But *that's* not it."

As Melissa smiles, Sarah is barely able to hold back her news, but is calculating how to get the biggest effect. While she waits, eyes wide, Sarah comes to sit facing on the creaky mattress and says, "Word has it Thomas' father is Jewish mafia!"

Sarah's tone of dread sends shivers of anxiety up Melissa's spine. "So he isn't just a small-time showoff—he's actually dangerous?"

Sarah sighs and slumps. "So we should stay out of his way. And not worry because whatever happens we'll always have each other."

Later, when Melissa leaves, she circles back to the campus as if it could provide the comfort of sanctuary. Entering the quad through the front gate, she makes her way through an ivy-covered walkway with arched leaded glass windows, and emerges in the courtyard where the summer Shakespeare plays will be put on. It is here that April will be singing with the Collegium Musicum, whose director was as surprised and impressed by her natural, pure soprano as were any of her friends.

Melissa climbs to the top of the last and highest row of the one section of seats that is already standing in the generous shade of a canopy formed by maple trees. She sits down. Her eyes trace the ivy. It seems to her that the campus has never been so lovely or so full of promise. Here, she and all her friends will learn how to set things right. For inspiration she decides to walk over to the conservatory, where she gazes at the thriving cycads, which, in their antiquity on Earth, represent the hallowed past of its evolving habitats. She then circles north, around George Beadle's corn patch, where he discovered the ancestral source of its cultivation in wild teosinte.

On impulse, she decides to visit Alan in his lab in the new Cummings Life Science Center which lies to the west of the quadrangle. She can see Cummings standing tall against the clear blue sky, towering over the bookstore and the old wing of the hospital. She has never been inside a basic science laboratory, and expects that it will inspire her with scenes of experiments designed to uncover the secrets of life. Next week when she begins work in the dog lab she may not have time to glimpse a purer and deeper form of biological science like biochemistry, biophysics, or the new science of molecular biology. She enters through the front door, stepping into the stainless steel elevator cab—which is sleeker than those in the hospital, and more like the newer ones in the loop—and then goes to the sixth floor to look for his lab.

As Melissa exits the elevator she turns right, taking note of the freshly buffed, highly waxed floor and the systematically numbered labs with scrupulously clean slate counter tops, large equipment, and intricate apparatuses of glass and plastic.

Several open doors reveal quiet atmospheres of concentration with soundtracks of soothing classical music. She sees water baths moving back and forth, massive centrifuges, petri dishes, and many pieces of specialized equipment that she can't identify. Each lab appears to have its own character, personality, and purpose: Some are busy and loud, some are full yet serene, and others are deserted and nearly dark.

After coming around to the elevator again, she makes another—but this time slower—circuit looking for Alan, and finds him alone in a darkened lab collecting glassware and loading it onto a wheeled steel cart. When he sees her he seems uncharacteristically glad as he stops and says brightly, "My grad student isn't here yet so I'm going to wash the glassware."

"Sounds like fun."

"Actually, I find it soothing. She can be a real *yenta!*"

Melissa laughs with Alan and follows him down the aisle on the inside of the building. To their right is a row of long slate counters, called lab benches, that end in an aisle lined by another work surface running along the length of the room beneath a long row of windows that rise all the way to the ceiling.

"What a building!"

"It's great. A new architect. Cutting edge."

"Are they working on the roof?"

Alan nods as he stops, opens the door of a dishwasher, and begins to remove dirty dishes from the cart, and to load them on the inside shelves of the machine.

"They're putting a huge P3 filter on the roof," Alan says authoritatively.

"Which is …?"

"It's designed to remove biohazards."

"Like …?"

"If something goes wrong with an experiment and researchers create or release a new pathogen, the filter will catch it."

"What might go wrong?"

"No one really knows."

"Then how can they be sure the filter will work?"

Alan shrugs. "I'm more worried about what's going on inside the lab. There's some kind of bacterial virus—that's a bacterio-phage—getting into all the cultures and the grad student is trying to pin it on me."

"Why?"

"She says I'm washing the glassware the wrong way."

"Isn't the machine washing them?"

"That's what I say! She's not what you'd call rational."

As Alan goes on about the grad student and the work of the lab, Melissa begins to get a colorful, earthy view of the realities of a lab, and her faith in science becomes a bit more grounded in the realization that things look better than they are—and that people are the same whether or not they are wearing white coats and using fancy equipment. The challenge of being human is here, too, in this temple to the discovery of hidden truth. Abruptly Alan goes quiet as an older woman enters the lab.

"Alan!"

"Yes!"

"Let's go!"

"Just finishing, want to get it right," he says, glancing at Melissa significantly.

Melissa introduces herself, then asks what's wrong.

The grad student, who has a long auburn braid, is wearing bug-eyed tortoiseshell glasses, tight jeans, and a baggy t-shirt with a picture of The Who. She does not introduce herself.

"The public shouldn't interfere with science! They're putting that stupid filter up because the neighbors are afraid of what we do in here. They should get that scientific progress has a cost. If a third of the population dies, that's just how it is!"

Melissa waits for a sign that she is joking, perhaps hazing or testing the help, but there is no sign of it as she goes on to talk about her physicist father's work with the Manhattan Project and the lessons he took away from the bombing of Hiroshima and Nagasaki. Melissa is shocked, but hides it well until she is able to leave.

Walking slowly to the bookstore, where she treats herself to a sandwich that she plans to take to a bench in the quadrangle, she remembers what she has heard about the alumni of the Manhattan Project, and wishes that those who had made the miraculous scientific breakthroughs that were used to feed the insatiable desire for destruction had not been blindsided by their managers, or that more had—like Oppenheimer—transformed their regrets into redemptive acts of peace. Melissa wonders if the University has done anything for life and love in the neighborhood or beyond. If so, she would like to know of it. She takes her lunch and sits next to the statue entitled "Why," and asks it all her heartfelt questions, feeling as helpless as Hamlet, whose scruples do nothing to mitigate the peril to his state.

Melissa is still absorbing the shocks of the morning as she dresses for dinner at the fancy restaurant downtown where she and Doug will meet his dad after work. As she and Doug ride north on the train, Doug watches the streets go by and keeps his thoughts to himself. He is uneasy and his mood pulls her in; she cheers herself by thinking of Sarah and of the ultimate truths toward which each and all of them—and all of life itself—are tending, like green shoots rising through the cracks of old cement.

By the time they reach the Perroquet, Melissa has restored her spirits with thoughts of the expansiveness of study and the possibility of discovery. This is fortunate for her as she and Doug feel a surge of synchronous, stressful alarm upon entering the imposing vestibule of the restaurant, which is more elegant than pretentious, and is so unlike places they frequent that they feel as if they've walked into another world where they are aliens. They squeeze between the potted ficus trees and the imposing podium over which a parrot-like maître de is glaring at them. A large man—presumably Doug's dad—strides toward them, arms out, as if he were Chairman of the Board. It occurs to Melissa that he may indeed own whatever workplace it is that he has just left behind. He puts his arm around Doug, and then punches his bicep, and says "Hey, hey, hey!"

"You look like a pair of fullbacks!" she says.

It must have been the right thing to say because he takes her hand, clasps it a bit too hard, and says, "So here's Missy, the girl with the spunk to get through a tight spot!"

"Thank you for helping us get a place to live," she replies, wondering what he means—until she recalls the motorcycle ride.

"Anything for my boy, and his friends."

The maître d's expression shifts as it is now clear they are with Doug's dad, and apparently in the power seat. Earlier, Melissa was glad to have had a dress; now she is sure that it is not dressy enough. As they follow the man to their table, she notes the décor, which is like the dinning room of an elderly woman who can no longer afford to light it as she would like. It is elegant, tasteful, and elaborate, not at all like the sleek Scandinavian designs that her parents and young friends prefer. When the elderly waiter arrives in his dark green vest and pleated pant uniform—giving them menus with an intrusive flourish, and bowing to Doug's father before welcoming them in a thick and possibly fake French accent—she longs for the warm and gracious ease of the car hops at the A&W near her home in Peoria. Looking around, the best feature of the restaurant seems to be the diners, who appear to be older, elegantly dressed, and well-mannered representatives of the old money set.

Within a few minutes, she becomes aware that Doug's dad does not seem to fit in any better than she or Doug. He is brash and clenched around some source of displeasure that is bringing out the clown in Doug, who apparently copes with his father's intensity by diverting his focus. Doug's dad, Mr. Post, puts up with this for a while, but by the time the main course arrives, he's done with the pretense of patience.

"What are the grades this quarter?"

As Doug tells him, Melissa is surprised. Although Doug has

feigned a lack of interest, he has proven his attentiveness with excellent grades. Then, when Mr. Post asks Melissa, her report is even better—all A's or A+'s, except for one A- in English. Mr. Post then frowns at Doug, whose glare catches Melissa unaware.

"This college costs a lot of money," Mr. Post asserts. "You have to get all you can out of it. You have to be the best. What summer position did you get?"

"I'm assisting a Nobel Prize-winning population biologist," Doug says, giving Melissa a keen look. She nods subtly to let him know that she recalls his asking her not to mention the professor's radical politics.

"Good, good," says Mr. Post. "And you?"

"I'm working in a dog lab in the medical school," she says, aiming to sound—accurately—as if she has a less prestigious job. She is surprised when Mr. Post gives her a look of disgust.

Turning to Doug, his father explains, "All a girl has to do is get her M.R.S. A man has to make himself. A man has to get ahead. It's an ugly bare-knuckled life in a tough and dirty city in a harsh world. You get to the top and marry money, or end up in a dog lab."

"Missy's going to be a doctor, Dad, maybe a surgeon," Doug smirks, with a wink at Melissa. Mr. Post looks shocked, and then revolted, until a light bulb goes on and his forehead relaxes under his balding hairline and the ego and money barriers fall. "Well, *there's* a new way to marry money."

As Melissa registers that he seems to be unprincipled, and unconcerned about it, Doug tells him, "We're not shacking up Dad, we're just friends who keep it simple by sharing expenses. She likes John, and I'm not committed."

"He's the smart one you talk about."

"And she studies with him."

Mr. Post looks confused. "And you shack—and you like him?"

"Everybody likes him," Melissa says.

"They're virgins, Dad."

Melissa stares at her plate while the confused Mr. Post relaxes, but keeps one eye on Doug as if worried that his son will think he's gone soft. Melissa senses that Mr. Post doesn't quite know what to do, and is confused by feeling sympathy for him personally, although at the same time wishing to be away from him. He is one of those who sees decay, criminality and conflict with the kind of cold eye that chills her. She makes the effort to forgive and to like him, and is glad in the end to be able to thank Mr. Post for a good dinner and for raising a son who has the gift of friendship.

Doug, apparently eager to de-stress, enters their apartment and goes directly to the kitchen for scotch. Melissa looks around to get more ideas for decorating. In a minute, Doug brings back two drinks on ice. She doesn't like scotch, but he is including her in a new way, so she takes one and sips it.

Suppressing a grimace, she says, "This room is as big as the apartment I grew up in!"

Doug laughs, assuming that she is exaggerating. She wonders if he sees that the apartment was once grand and retains something of its old elegance. The high trim, ornate metal fixtures, and classic tiles lend the front room, central hall, four bedrooms, dining room, and kitchen with servant's room an air of faded gentility. They intend to use the servant's room for storage, but if they have trouble making rent they can find another roommate who is content with a single bed and rod for hanging clothes. The walls, all yellow paint over old wallpaper, and the patched white ceilings are cheerful and fresh enough to leave alone. April and

Alan, who will be going home for most of the summer, can add what they like when they move in.

"Do you know where they're staying?"

"They're probably shacking up and hiding it."

"From us?"

"From themselves."

"I didn't realize they had … you know."

"They didn't want you to."

Melissa hopes that she is hiding her shock. April used to confide in Melissa, the only other girl she knew who was a virgin and wasn't ashamed to admit it. Now Melissa may be the only one.

As if reading her mind, Doug says, "Yup. You and John are the only holdouts now—and who knows about him. Alaska's lousy with prostitutes."

"Prostitutes! Surely not John. He wouldn't have to pay someone. He's very … lots of women would want him."

Doug snorts. "You don't pay because no one wants you, you pay to avoid having strings attached."

Melissa is almost crying as she says, "You mean to avoid feelings and responsibility?"

"To avoid Alan's situation."

"What do you mean?"

"The parents are about as happy as Romeo and Juliet's. And they're years from graduating and earning an income. They're going to end up having to choose between disaster and heartbreak."

Melissa sighs, "That's just them."

"Wouldn't you be the same?"

"You know I would. That's why I don't go out. But if a man uses a woman that way, doesn't it change him?"

"Sadly, no," Doug says with a smirk.

There is a knock at the door, allowing Melissa to escape what has been a disturbing conversation for one so sexually innocent, and so averse to chaos and darkness.

"Who is it?"

Moments later Sarah enters, laughing, followed by a large group of friends that includes Anne, Greg, Randall, the two women from the morning house meeting, and several other older students whom Melissa does not recognize. After welcoming them warmly, she sits down on her pillow while Doug starts a conversation about going to the Checkerboard or the Queen Bee, or to a nightclub up on Clark Street north of Old Town.

"May I join you?" says a polite male voice.

Melissa looks up to see Randall, who has never sought her out and to whom she has never said more than a few words at a time. She has, perhaps, avoided him because of his reputation for promiscuity.

"Sure," she says unenthusiastically.

"You're one of those quiet ones, aren't you," he says as he pulls up a floor pillow next to her while the others follow Doug on a tour of the apartment. She bristles at being typed and then relents. He is being kind, open, and charming; not needling or challenging her as Doug sometimes does when others are around.

"What quiet ones?"

Randall leans on one elbow and stretches out his long body with easy sensuality. "One of those who is quiet and humble and ignored and who suddenly runs away with the prize."

"Prize?"

"I know you studied with John, but I didn't know you were as smart. Sarah told me."

"Told you what?"

"About how well you do. I don't read Midwesterners very well. I thought you were ... *with* John."

"Oh! I see. Well, we're both dyed-in-the-wool Midwesterners, and innocents in certain ways, which is probably the reason we're so close. But he's not my boyfriend. I've ... been concentrating on school."

She examines Randall's open face. She finds no trace of a smooth operator or calculator in search of conquests, or of dislike or dominance. She asks skeptically, "You like smart women?"

"I like the art of conversation. I like getting to know new kinds of people. And I'm used to talking to my mother, who is one of the smartest people I know."

"Well then," she says with a sly smile, holding out her hand to shake his, "it's nice to finally meet you properly, Randall Noll."

As they shake hands, she notices his is warm and dry, with a firm pressure that is confident without overdoing it. She puts her worries behind her as they talk about last quarter's classes, and their plans for the summer and the next academic year. Like Alan, he is taking a summer course, which, in Randall's case, is a math course to make up for one he lacked in high school. He is also Jewish, which surprises her as Alan is proud of looking Jewish and she has come to expect all Jews to look like him. Randall is from L.A. and looks it: He is always tan, the hair on his head, chest, and arms is bleached blond, presumably by the sun, and his relaxed west-coast manner is the opposite of the high energy volubility that Alan brought with him from New York—but is slowly losing.

As they talk, Melissa realizes that Randall isn't at all what she expected. He is curious, interesting, poised and yet natural, attentive and good company. She is soon at ease again and enjoying herself. She is liking him more and more, too, as if making a new best friend, and cannot get enough of his gaze, which is open and free at rest but may turn suddenly sharp or empathetic. She is enjoying herself so much that she does not think of the others until she sees that the group is leaving, and that Sarah and Doug are not with them. As she sees them out, she asks Anne, "Where's Sarah?"

Anne rolls her eyes and heads for the stairs, turning back once to give Melissa a withering glance. Melissa closes the door and returns to Randall with a puzzled look. "Did you see Sarah leave? Or Doug?"

Randall replies, "They're in his room."

"What, together?" she asks, the distress of the day returning.

"Didn't see it coming?"

Melissa shakes her head and stares at the floor, her feelings in tumult. After a long pause she smiles ruefully and says, "I'm not ready for the big wide world."

"Who is?" he asks kindly. "That's why we're here."

She smiles and nods, greatly comforted, and then stands. "How about a walk?"

"Shall we go to the Medici?"

"Sure."

Later, after they've had coffee, and Randall has walked her home, he pauses at the front door, and asks casually, "There's an Indian restaurant on Oak Street that I've been wanting to try, would you like to join me tomorrow night?"

"I'd love it," she replies shyly before disappearing up the stairs, through the apartment door, and down the hall to her room, where she closes the door and dives under the covers with a pillow wrapped around her ears in case Sarah and Doug are still together down the hall.

She thinks for a while about her virginity, of how much she has valued and appreciated it, and of how it now seems to be a source of difference and division. Sarah and April both concealed their sexual lives from her, while both Doug and Randall remain opaque to her. Worse, she has no knowledge or understanding of the act itself; she knows that the penis breaks the hymen, but cannot imagine how such a floppy organ could do such a thing. She does not know how to do it, or even how to let a man do it to her. She has only ever touched her privates while showering, or by accident after going to the toilet.

She has met Randall at just the right time. He is wonderfully kind and experienced, and doesn't mind her company at all. They might even come to like each other very much, and to care for each other as more than friends. She thinks back on the way he looked at her, how he seemed to see all of her while turning away from none of it. If he wants to take her to bed, she will say yes.

10

The West

John pulls his head deeper into the sleeping bag, trying to forget the nightmare that woke him, the rocky ground under his back, and the headache that is gripping him in the thin, biting air. But he can't forget. Every time he closes his eyes, unwanted images appear of a lush alpine meadow ringed by crumbling six-flats and rusting skyscrapers that cast shadows over rats and rapists. John is almost wistful for his Alaskan cannery dreams, where he skinned fish all night with occasional glimpses of Glacier Bay and dense, moss-covered evergreen forests draped in ferns, lichens, and fungi.

He analyzes the nightmare to break its spell. It may mean he dreads returning to school; or it could be a cautionary tale from his chafed feet and shoulders, which are balking at carrying a sixty-pound pack on the rough hike that began yesterday with a walk six miles in and thirty-five hundred feet up. In a few hours, he will continue to the summit of Long's Peak. John can endure the pain, a small price to pay for sleeping in the lap of a great peak, but he is running out of patience with Bill, the out-of-shape trip leader who puffed malevolently up the trail bragging about his conquests of all but three of Colorado's fourteeners, while venting his temper at John.

The only reason John believes he can achieve the summit

is that his new friend and mentor Grady, a graduate student in physics with a passion for the outdoors, told John he could do it. Grady has been edgy with exertion, too, but is taking time to enjoy the unfolding beauty of the magnificent ascent. Even Bill's fidgety little brother Dean—who trained with Grady at altitude this summer—was able to scamper up the sparsely carpeted earth like a bighorn sheep, pausing at off-trail viewpoints as if to search for succulent clumps of grass hidden in fissures or behind crests.

John, inspired by Dean and Grady's unflagging support, had finally felt comfortable enough to talk back to Bill, who sounded irritable at lunch the day before when he said, "You'd better eat everything you've got or you're going to lose what little muscle you have."

After returning the jab with "I'd better eat yours then, that's not muscle holding up your hip belt," Bill had stopped speaking to him. John was relieved because it was all he could do to keep his feet on the uneven trail. Biting his cheeks in pain, he had actually been thinking of turning back when the trail finally flattened and Grady spotted the stone hut below the Keyhole—a huge notch in the northwest shoulder of the peak.

As Grady and Dean had sped ahead to set up camp in the Boulder Field, John needed to catch his breath while he stared in awe. Then, when Bill had caught up and pointed out in a flat voice that they should have seen a ranger by now, John grasped that he was, for the first time, in the wild.

As that memory returns, his nightmare finally dissipates and he is able to smile at the tent roof snapping in the wind above his nose. Feeling nature enveloping him in her logic, dwarfing the artificiality of school and the depravity of the city's behavioral sink, he realizes he is at the source—that perilous place of freedom that gives rise to dreams as well as nightmares. He laughs, but silently, to avoid waking Grady.

But the laugh sticks in John's throat as he realizes that with freedom comes daunting responsibility: If anything happens to any of them now, they will have to deal with it on their own.

After years of celebrating Thanksgiving, and imagining that he admired self-reliance, John finally understands the kind of crazy courage the Pilgrims had to have had to cross the North Atlantic on their way to the terrifying splendor of the American wilderness. He sees, for the first time, that the price of freedom is accepting responsibility for everyone and anything—and he is ready to pay it. This recognition releases a rush of confidence greater than the one he felt when he first belayed.

John's mind tires and wanders back to the trail. Caught between remembering and dreaming, he sees a hawk riding a current of air, stands of open pine forest, distant dark green slopes, and monumental massifs. He sees gritty yellowish soil on gray rock holding tenacious trailside lichens and silvery succulents. He sees expansive meadows dotted with late-blooming flowers, marsh grasses, and black pools reflecting deep blue skies and scattered clouds. Every wrinkle in the rock and every fallen fragment is a wonder that opens secrets to John's willing eyes.

The next thing John knows, Grady is shaking his bag in the pre-dawn dark and handing him a Sierra cup full of lukewarm oatmeal and raisins. John eats slowly and gropes for his daypack, glad that the weather held, and that they will be able to leave most of their gear in the tents.

All too soon, they are following Grady up the trail, navigating by the light of his jerky flashlight, which is when John becomes fully awake. When they start clambering breathlessly up boulders on all fours, his focus narrows and heightens, and his balance sharpens.

They attain the rocky gap of the Keyhole at dawn, and look out on a stunning panorama of pink-tinged peaks. Anxious to return before the afternoon thunderstorms, they move on immediately, following Grady south on a series of windy, vertiginous ledges, where John is grateful for the generous footing. When they reach the trough extending up from Glacier Gorge, John takes the lead up a several-hundred-foot scramble and stops at a rope left in place by a previous climber. As Bill objects that purists shouldn't use it, and Grady argues that it prevents destruction of the route by rock-crumbling pitons, John takes hold of the rope and slithers up around the chockstone to take the level ground.

After a brief, dizzying fear that his head will crack like an eggshell far below, John takes his first southward view of Rocky Mountain National Park, the wilderness beyond, and the gray stone peaks that roll away to the horizon like choppy waves on a sea of land. He forgets his headache, his aching feet, and his stiff muscles, giving himself up to awe of a scene that seems unreal.

It takes only a few minutes for the grandeur to put his piddly human problems into perspective, and for him to understand that nothing in his life is as real as this. While the others are still arguing at the chockstone, John approaches the Narrows, which drives everything from his mind but balance and fear as this traverse is more exposed on both sides than he could have imagined or prepared for.

On his left, and also on his right, the earth falls away. The horizontal surfaces below may be hundreds of feet down, or thousands, but he is afraid to look in order to make a closer guess. When he puts a foot out, he feels like a spider suspended on a web, except a spider has silk and adhesive force, whereas he has nothing but his weight and the hard soles of his heavy boots. If he falls, he will accelerate at thirty-two feet per second per second until he hits rock. His body will be crushed and his head may splatter.

Nothing in John's experience has prepared him to face this possibility. His attention and concentration become intense. His will focuses on the Narrows. His eyes avoid the precipices to the right and left, keeping to the trail just ahead, seeking out the best places to place his feet one careful, and relaxed, step at a time. Fear blocks out the abysses on either side, and then recedes. Body and mind know nothing but the task at hand.

When John reaches the other side, he turns and waits for the others, who file silently across the homestretch. A few minutes later, they are standing on the summit in a daze as wind deafens their ears, tears at their clothes, and freezes their scalps through their knit hats. John turns his mind from discomfort to savor his first real accomplishment in the world. His previous successes were all achieved on paper, at desks, or in classrooms. No matter what happens now, he will always have the memory of this tangible, inarguable victory over himself in harsh surroundings.

When each man has had his moment of solitary reckoning, the group spends a full ten minutes celebrating with backslapping, picture taking and landmark spotting. Noting that Bill isn't scolding him for having taken the lead at the chockstone, John realizes that he has gained—or rather seized—a new level of respect from these mentors. And when they are ready to descend, he waits courteously for Grady and Bill to begin, which fills him with the curious power of choosing to follow rather than lead.

The descent turns out to be far more difficult than the ascent. It takes fewer calories, but demands a lot more care and courage.

Looking down and away from the slope, he cannot lean into the rock, steady himself with his hands, or plan a fall. When John becomes unsure of his feet, he turns over and scrambles backward, his belly near the rock, his hands ready to grab hold.

At the keyhole, they stop to take one last, grand view of Glacier Gorge and the approaching clouds, and hurry back down to the Boulder Field. As the four newly close friends pack their gear, arguing pleasantly about whether they saw Fort Collins or Nederland from the summit, John is relaxed, giddy, and exhausted. They continue their descent rapidly, and, in Dean's case, carelessly. He is full of energy, still moving along like a bighorn sheep, and now sometimes hopping on one foot from the inside of the trail to the outside. Bill, who is walking behind, seems too exhausted to rein in his little brother.

Finally, fatigue catches up with Dean and he makes a mistake. While the rest are finishing lunch beside a dry waterfall, Dean jumps toward a boulder, slips on the gravel, and disappears down a steep incline feet first. His impact is dull and anticlimactic, no louder than the thumping of a dog's tail, but the other three men drop their lunches and rush to the edge of the dry fall to peer down at least twenty feet below. John is still hoping irrationally that Dean really does have the qualities of a mountain goat, and will come gamboling up again, but he is lying still, his body spread-eagled limply beside a boulder. John, Grady and Bill scramble to the bottom, where they find Dean dazed but conscious, his right foot stuck under the boulder at an odd angle. John spots a gaping hole in Dean's leg that opens around a splintered bone and a tiny gusher of blood.

Grady turns white and staggers to one side, his hands on his knees, head dangling. Bill kneels next to Dean, grabs his arm, and says with desperate bravado, "You're going to be okay. You're going to be okay. It isn't bad. It isn't bad." John feels a weird kind of calm. He took first aid as part of a Red Cross water rescue class and knows exactly what to do. While Bill begins to blubber, John applies pressure to Dean's femoral artery and tells Grady to look away, take off his flannel shirt, and tear it into strips.

John takes the strips, wraps them around Dean's thigh, and uses the carabiner that Grady always wears on his wrist to tighten the strips into a tourniquet. The leg stops bleeding. As Bill finally takes a deep breath, John tells him to get some tree branches for a stretcher. While Bill is distracted by the task of searching and cutting, John has Grady fetch two sticks. When Grady returns, John pulls the broken leg straight, Dean bites on one stick, and Grady splints the leg with the other.

When Bill returns with a few thorny shrubs he is holding like a bouquet, Grady grabs his Swiss Army knife and darts up the trail. He returns almost immediately with two large branches, and then rushes off again and returns with more. John takes off his belt and begins to weave it all together into a crude frame. Grady and Bill begin to help more effectively, gathering and weaving branches and bungee cords until the stretcher is ready. Then they wrap it tightly in a tent and divvy up Dean's pack so each can take a third of its weight.

They place Dean on the rickety stretcher, cover him with a rain fly, and race-walk him down the mountain, taking it in turns to carry the heavy stretcher. They could not have carried half as much before the injury, but now do what they must. The descent is rough on all of them, especially Dean, who groans with every lurch. A thousand yards down, John realizes he can't remember how long a tourniquet can be left in place without risking loss of limb, and also that he didn't check the time when he applied it. He stops the group and replaces the tourniquet with a pressure dressing, which gives them all a minute's rest.

It seems to take forever, but they make it down in an hour and a half. They find a ranger at the station who rushes Dean to a clinic in Estes Park. The other three follow in Bill's Travelall, hoping silently that all will be well. Just as they arrive at the clinic, Dean is whisked away, and they sit down to the hardest ordeal of the day, which is waiting to see if Dean will lose that leg.

After what seems like hours, the doctor comes out to tell them that Dean will be fine. Bill, his clammy hands shaking with relief, rushes to call his parents. Grady and John get up and go to the window, which has a fine view of the park. Grady punches John in the arm and takes his neck in the crook of his arm. The two horse around until the last of their nervous energy is gone, and then fall asleep in waiting room chairs.

11

Dog Days

Doug lays on his left arm, right leg dangling off his stool as a counterbalance, disheveled hair flat against the cold slate, and stares at the column that has been running for thirty-five and three quarters of the past thirty-six hours. Having started it night before last at midnight, he didn't want to miss the finish. He has been running columns since the funding for population studies fell through before he got to do anything interesting. It's probably just as well. A drip-drip-drip of math might have driven him mad; this protein extraction is easy, and doesn't interfere with his real life, as he has come to think of it—the partying and gaming and women and going out on the town. The only catch is that the job is boring, boring, boring. They would have to pay him big bucks to get him to do this for a living. He is here for the air conditioning—which is the thought that leads to the biggest epiphany of his still-young college career.

If anyone were looking at him—which no one is because this newly space-rich lab is empty this Saturday morning at the end of August—they would see only a faint crooked smile. Behind that smile, he knows this is a life-changing moment: He is going to give up the doctoring plan and get himself ready for the "B" school— the business center that is cashed up and gradually stealing the shine of the poorer elements of the campus that count their riches in Nobel Laureates, or other signs of adulation from their peers.

Doug wants money. His dad is right. He should make it, and marry it. Dad's fulfilled and Mom's happy enough, but Dad is the original rebel without a cause—he doesn't follow anyone, and no one tells him what to do. And no one can stop him because he sees through things and gets his own way. And he gives more money to charity than anyone else Doug knows. He can't stand people stepping on the little guy; he used to be the little guy, and now, in his heart of hearts, he wants everyone to be the big guy, and firmly believes that every man on Earth can have his way. Doug carries on the family faith in the win-win, and knows now that wasting his life away in a lab extracting protein fractions is no win for him. His grad student loves it, and can't see why Doug doesn't, which is just one more good reason to quit this game before he learns to like it.

When Doug has captured his last protein fractions in tubes, labeled them carefully, put them away, and cleaned up his bench, he goes out walking the streets to try on his new aspiration. He heads to 53rd street to see what he can see in the businesses of Hyde Park.

His dad settled into the commodities market after a varied career, but that is not something Doug will do. He wants to create something real that has nothing to do with gambling on agriculture or the weather, or with the win-lose mentality of manufacturing. He also wants to do something of his own that belongs to his generation, something new and better that adds value which is commensurate with profit.

By the time Doug heads east on 53rd Street he has ruled out sales and services—his at least—and the public sector. As he passes Harold's Chicken Shack on the left with its bullet-proof customer windows, the hardware store on the right with its bars, and Beaulieu's with the terrible Miss Taylor, the facing rows of shops and eateries seem to him like prison cells lining a corridor. Each is too small; he would get claustrophobia. He needs a bigger, friendlier field of play. When he finally reaches the bank with the big clock opposite the IC tracks, and goes in to peruse the row of tellers and office doors behind them, he realizes how confined they are and rules out management. He turns back, a bit discouraged from the lack of inspiration and vision, but reminds himself that he has three more years of college, then business school, and a few years of paid experience during which he can figure it all out and find his place in life. He has been meaning to try LSD, maybe that will put him on the fast track, and thinks Greg has some, or may have some.

Doug stops at Sarah's, but they are all out. He continues south, wending his way through the buildings east of the quad, then down into the basement where he sees the huge stone bull and Egyptian tomb relics of the Oriental Institute. He continues on through the Robie House gift shop, back to Rockefeller Chapel, then around and through, eventually ending up in a low, open brick building where he has never been. Inside, he sees older students lined up holding stacks of cards, while across the room a special typewriter punches tiny rectangular holes in fresh, blank cards. They seem to be like the test forms he has used, but in physical form. The student at the front of the line steps up and places a huge stack of them in the reader. A moment later, the card reader whirrs, and the student moves to the side to wait. A teaching assitant calls out the name of another waiting student and hands him a printed sheet. After hearing the student sigh with relief, Doug intercepts him before he reaches the door.

"What is that?"

"It's the computer printout. Look at this! It took me hours to type the cards right for it to solve an equation that I could have solved in minutes. Stupid."

"Homework?"

"Learning to use the card reader. What a pain."

The annoyed student exits, but Doug is thrilled. It's no pain to him, and a light has gone on in his mind. Standing with his arms crossed as he watches the students tangle with the card reader, he remembers watching a spacewalk on TV and visiting Cape Canaveral; then thinks back to the time he went to San Francisco with his father for a sales pitch at the defense contractor Fairchild, where his dad thought having his technology-dazzled son tagging along wouldn't hurt.

A computer at the university? He hadn't ever heard of it. Sure it's a pain now, and will continue to challenge anyone who's working at the cutting edge, but he sees that it's a way of bringing the space age down to Earth—and that it probably won't be going away. As he walks back to Sarah's, he is tingling all over as his gut shouts, "YES!"

He now knows where he is going, and that the playing field will be like a moving walkway—it will just keep rolling, and there will be plenty of space on it for everyone to participate in creating a new world. He can't wait.

Sarah stalks up the hallway from Doug's bedroom. Melissa wakes, sees that it's after midnight, and rushes out after her to ask, "Do you want to stay in my room?"

Sarah stops, balls up her fists, and shakes her head. When she opens the front door, Melissa catches up, stops her, and says calmly, "Don't go out alone now, it isn't safe! I'll come with you."

While waiting for Melissa to dress, Sarah is too relieved to be angry with her. As they leave, Melissa, blessedly, says nothing. Sarah knows she is lucky that Melissa was in, and is glad to be walking down the middle of the street with her to the Golden Rectangle, where there will be white security phones on every corner.

Eventually Sarah calms down and feels sheepish, saying, "Sorry to be so much trouble."

"What did he do?"

"He—we—got into a weird pattern. I have no idea what to do about it. I walk out when he starts needling me, but after a while he shows up and I just can't say no."

"So, like a love-hate thing?"

"Like an S&M thing."

"What's S&M?"

"The sex is amazing. It's like an addiction. We start out fine, and then it's the best thing ever, and then we find ways to make it even better—more and more exciting, and one of those is aggression. We arouse each other by tussling, verbally or physically."

"Randall arouses me with conversation. Maybe you could try that."

Sarah snorts. "That wouldn't work for either of us."

"There must be something fun, or that feels good."

"Climax feels good."

"Isn't amazing good enough?"

"Yes, but he feels safer, and I do too, when we can feel like it won't last. It's too soon, too ... scary."

"I would be more scared of the pattern than of the breakup. You will break up, you know."

"Maybe we're afraid of that. Aren't you?"

"I love Randall, but I don't really get him. Not deep down. It's like we're opposites that attract, and we open each other's worlds, but it isn't … home. It's a life changing thing, and it's enough, more than enough. We're like … soul mates."

"So are we, but it's scary, and confusing, like a trapeze act without a net."

"Well, if you ever want to come to my room, or you want me to walk with you, I will. But promise me you won't do anything on impulse. It's dangerous. And *he* should walk you home. He's the big guy who's supposed to protect us. I'm going to talk with him about that."

"Don't. Let me do it. We'll figure something out. It isn't fair to you. Part of it now is it's just so hot."

The night is not only muggy, it's also full of phantoms. Sarah follows Melissa's darting eyes into the shadows beyond the sidewalk on either side and recognizes that someone with hostile intentions could easily spring out from behind one of the cars parked bumper to bumper along the curbs of every block they pass. And, walking out at 1:00 a.m. on a weeknight means that the people they encounter are less likely to be friendly. The quiet was soothing at first, but now she is worried. They are both relieved when they make it to her house without incident and, because Sheryl is away, they are free to talk a little until Missy goes to sleep. Sarah lays awake pondering the unstable excitements of her affair with Doug, and the thorny office politics at NORC, which fade to trivial in comparison.

Randall can't resist a love affair. Each one has been different, and each one has changed his life. He expects them to be predictable, but in each case he has found himself in a wilderness with no map but the Torah and its body of ethics. He is grateful to have it as a guide, and even more grateful that gentile women appreciate Jewish men who intend to give them pleasure, and who know how to do it. With Melissa, the first entry was difficult, and she bled and cried unexpectedly, but he has since redeemed himself by broadening and intensifying and varying her orgasms.

He has, literally, made love. He is in love with her for her conversation and for the delight she takes in him; and she is in love with him for what they share. But she isn't like the others. He doesn't possess her; she doesn't idolize or use him. She challenges him. She works his mind as he works her body. It is exciting and heady for both of them. But he does not have her full attention when they are not in bed. Part of her mind is elsewhere, and so, now, is his. It will make the breakup easier when they finally come to their senses.

In the meantime, they have become great friends. He can easily believe—or, rather, choose to believe—that John is her best friend. In that way, she is one of the guys, but better because her interests are different than his and more varied. The class difference is part of it. She earned her way here while he was given it. He does well in school, of course, but has done little else. She knows a side of the world that he does not—and vice versa of course. And both of them know more about the city now than they knew they wanted to.

Thanks to her they go to the Maxwell Street Market. There they both think they can smell the stockyards, which closed long ago but are said to have left a lingering smell. They take the bus to "avoid buying back their hubcaps," as the saying has it, and taste beef barbecued over a fire in a trashcan, and ladyfinger pecans sold by a big black man who brings them up from the south. These are more delicious and affordable than anything else he has eaten in Chicago, which has helped him to realize for the first time that money and value can be strangers to one another, and that it will be up to him to seek out value. They have also enjoyed dim sum in a back alley of Chinatown, chicken with a very hot sauce from the chicken shack, and Irish stew at a lunch counter on the magnificent mile near the bridge over the Chicago River.

Thanks to him they've eaten at Indian restaurants all over town, heard all kinds of local music in small clubs, been to the ballet, to the Steppenwolf Theater, the symphony in Grant Park, and to Lavinia Park—summer home of the Chicago Symphony. Best of all, he has taken her to his cousin's apartment in the Hancock Building when his cousin was away. They drank a bottle of Champagne, got tipsy on the view, and had sex in every room until they collapsed and slept until noon on Sunday. They go to the Art Institute every week, where they always stop to see the Impressionists, and where Randall is able to share his love of painting with a neophyte. They have, as Greg put it, made each other cross-cultural and cross-class.

He has also turned her onto Judaism, and that's when he wondered if she might be the one. She doesn't love it because she loves him; she is drawn to it as strongly as if she were truly a member of a lost tribe. She is prime marriage material and his open-minded parents would love her, but he feels uneasy about this. He is not ready to be faithful, and probably won't be for years, and she expects fidelity.

He would like to let the affair run its natural course, but they are already deeply attached and he may have to break with her before it peaks and ebbs. He is not sure. He will wait and see if he begins to feel committed, in which case he will have no choice but to break up. But for now, he is content to enjoy going out to places that he would never have gone on his own.

12

Fall

I t's the Friday before the start of fall quarter classes, and Melissa has come to the gym to work out. While home for the September break, she realized that she had been missing dance and gymnastics, so when she got back a week ago she visited Ida Noyes Hall and Bartlett Gym, where she spotted a few men working out on rings and parallel bars. Below the equipment lay thick mats that could be used for floor exercise.

The high ceilings, arched leaded glass windows, and Neo-Gothic architecture of the gymnasium give it the look of a museum for outdated equipment with new mats.

Melissa feels awkward working out in the gym in the old leotard and tights that reveal everything about her body, including her lack of fitness. As she warms up, however, and her flexibility and strength return, she rediscovers the joy of stretching and dancing. It has been so long that the exercises feel new, stimulating, and invigorating. Then she walks on her hands, does front and back walkovers, somersaults, tinsikas, and cartwheels. She is not in shape to do handsprings, nor is there enough room, but she doesn't mind. For now at least, the warm-ups are enough.

Melissa sits on a mat and takes a break, looking around to see if she knows any of the other students who have come in. She checks the smattering of men who are trying valiantly to master feats of prowess on the high bar, parallel bars, or horse. She watches the man on the opposite wall who is wearing a sleeveless T-shirt and gym shorts and hanging by his fingertips. As he traverses a ledge ten feet above the floor, she smiles, realizing that he is literally—rather than figuratively—climbing the walls. As he moves gracefully toward the window, she becomes entranced, and stares in wonder as he begins to do pull-ups, and then one-armed pull-ups, and then fingertip pull-ups. His clearly defined muscles ripple out in high relief on his back and arms. It is an impressive display of physical power, but it is his way of moving that transports her. When he releases the wall, lands cat-like on the wooden floor, and turns to the side to talk to his companion, she realizes with a shock that it is John.

She pivots away in confusion, overwhelmed by inchoate feelings. She tries to think them through. He is her best friend. But his body has changed, and arouses her passion. No male body has ever possessed her like that. The idea in her head that John is smart and Randall is sexy falls apart. She likes both of them. She loves both of them. But she is going out with Randall.

She hopes that John has not noticed her yet. She is all but naked. She heads toward the door as if she has not seen him and walks—not too slow, not too fast—toward the women's locker room.

As John is doing his finger pull-ups, Grady says, "Take it easy, John. You're not at Yosemite. You're not even at Devil's Lake."

John drops down again to the floor. "I'm just cranked up." He looks over to find Missy just in time to see her disappear through the door to the hallway inside. He sees her body in his mind's eye, the shape of her breasts in motion, the perfection of her thighs, the curve of her hips, the narrow triangle between the tops of her legs. He sits abruptly and leans forward to do a painful stretch in hopes of hiding his erection and ending it.

"That's enough for me," Grady says, perhaps aware of John's predicament. "See you in the shower."

John has been thinking of Melissa all summer, especially while working in the cannery where the machines took constant vigilance. Despite the monotony and overpowering smell of fish, he would imagine that she was there as she always had been in the library, sitting nearby, comforting him with her faith and strengthening him with her focus. On the drive though Yellowstone, Beartooth Pass, and Glacier, he would imagine, especially as he was falling asleep, that he was sharing with her the awestruck exhilaration he felt when encountering the wild. He even thought of her when he was thinking of the girls who sliced the fish, and who might have attracted him if they had more energy left at the end of their fourteen-hour days.

The memories of machines and fish have relaxed his desire, so he hurries to catch up with Grady, who is already gone, and with Melissa, who may be ready to have lunch across the street at the Blue Gargoyle Café in the Unitarian Church, which serves new foods like whole grain bread.

As John emerges breathlessly from the locker room, Melissa pretends that she did not see him before, and allows herself to be swept away by his vitality. She is both excited and anxious when he asks her to lunch, but soon they are catching up and joking in the old way—but perhaps more warmly—and swapping stories about their summer work. They go inside the low, ornate entrance to the row of serving tables and choose sandwiches, drinks, and snacks. They go on into the sanctuary, where they find a quiet table away from the small crowd.

"It's another world in here, isn't it?" Melissa asks as she

reads scriptural passages that speak of love on colorful banners surrounded by flowers. She peruses the architecture, which echoes the other older buildings of the university, and the dark seats that blend in with the shadowy recesses of the modest-sized interior.

"Yes. It's been years since I was in church. Couldn't sit still."

Melissa smiles and says boldly, "So you went away a boy and came back a man. What did it?"

John smiles as he tells her about his adventures, more or less in order. She listens, spellbound, as he speaks to all of her as never before, and their thoughts and feelings join to create a world all their own. When his hand brushes hers accidentally their bodies freeze, their gazes lock, and in that moment she knows that she loves him passionately—more than she could love Randall because she is John, and John is she. They are one soul and one mind in continuing dialogue. She has never been so happy, or so dismayed.

"What about your summer?" he asks. When she tells him about her compulsive washing, the strong and lingering odor of the dogs and the creeping meaninglessness of their last breaths, he nods and mentions the hours and hours of watching fish flesh enter a can and smelling the filleting table and the basins of offal. She concludes by saying with sudden resolution, "Someday I'm going to go west and stay there."

"Me too. I want to go to medical school in the Northwest."

"Me too. Oregon. Portland."

"Yes."

As they leave, Melissa asks with an unreasonable pang of jealousy, "Did you … go out with anyone?"

"I spent time with a couple of women at the cannery. One talked all the time and said nothing, and one was lonely. Nice, but nothing in common."

They exit and head north toward their apartments. He takes her hand and suddenly swings her toward him and kisses her. Her body responds. He says, "I should have done that before I left."

"Yes, yes, we should have! But John, I don't know what to do, I spent time with someone too."

He turns to one side, face drawn into an expression of upset that she has never seen, and that makes her afraid as well as miserably torn. "Who?"

"Randall," she confesses.

John looks incredulous and contemptuous. "The Randall who'll sleep with anyone? That Randall?"

"That isn't fair. You don't know him."

"He knew how I felt about you!"

"What?"

"I … I knew how I felt that night after we went to see Dizzy, when you came to my room."

"You knew and didn't say?"

"Your reaction was … I didn't know what to do. I took Doug's advice and pretended it was nothing."

"Doug knows. And Sarah. Everyone but me! I wish, well, to be perfectly frank, I'm glad to know more now than I did before. I might never have known what I feel for you."

John shakes his head. He cannot look at her. He swings his gym bag over his shoulder as if to leave but he can't. He's stuck.

"Do you want me to break up with him? Or, do you … think badly of me?"

When he shakes his head and grunts, she says. "We didn't have an understanding. Don't tell me you see me as untrue, or as used goods."

"I don't know how to live with this."

He strides away fast, and begins to run as she begins to cry. He runs faster and faster, pausing impatiently for traffic and running in place until he can run again; until he is winded and in pain and unaware of anything but his burning muscles and surging breath. He has gone all the way to Beaulieu's and into the line, where he sloshes black coffee into a cup and slaps it on the tray with a sliver of sweet potato pie.

Jerome watches John. He does not sense danger and can see from the sweat running down in front of John's ears and his panting that he has run off steam; even so, the last thing Jerome wants in his restaurant is a man who is like an unexploded land mine that might be triggered by the smallest and most innocuous of incidents. He is used to defusing anger, and is also used to acting the wide-eared bartender and surrogate father to the youth who frequent his place in search of stability and kindness. It will be easy to calm a good-natured customer in a nearly empty dinning room.

When John stops distractedly in front of Jerome to pay, eyes wandering everywhere and nowhere, he adopts his cool voice and says lightly on the upbeat, "Hey, little brother, what's happening?"

After a pause he catches John's eyes with a warm gaze that finally draws his attention.

John's focus comes in laser sharp, and his face breaks into a sheepish look. "I don't know, man, I don't even know."

He sighs, then pays, and with a half-nod takes his tray and finds a seat in the corner where he can stare at the wall. He feels strangely heavy, and is comforted by the pie, which he eats in a few bites. Then he sips his coffee and tries to gather his wits by pondering a math problem that he may have missed on last spring's final. He sits until the last of the coffee is cold and he can smell his own coffee breath.

Jerome comes over to where John is sitting and tries to read the young man, who looks to him like one sad mother.

"John! You okay?"

John looks up at Jerome standing by his side with a gaze that is empty of hope—a look that Jerome knows all too well. He sits down opposite John, a rare act that Miss Taylor ignores after he nods to her, an even rarer act of tacit approval that means she'll let it go and not give him grief about it. When John looks at Jerome with a confused look, Jerome senses heartache.

"Trouble with family? A girl?

John frowns, still barely able to think. "A girl. A woman, now."

"Do you want her?"

John is taken by surprise. He has not looked at it that way. The answer is easy.

"Yes. Forever."

Jerome smiles in his mind. Forever is a long time, but at John's age might mean longer than he can see into the future, which might be a few months.

"Then what you doin' here?"

John's eyes come alive. He smiles slightly, and shakes his head.

"Good question, big brother."

Jerome smiles widely, eyes sparkling with kindness, and goes back to his seat at the till.

13

Tangle

S arah is frustrated with her friendship group, which seems hell-bent on implosion, and with herself for failing to get them to see how lucky they are to have formed such strong bonds for so young, diverse, and intense a set of rapidly changing and continually challenged young adults. She is tempted to give up on them, or on her dream of becoming a leader and connector who can guide a group of talented and strong-willed souls to discover the best version of itself, the kind who can transform antagonism into synergy. But it is too soon to give up on all this potential.

Maybe it is her time to grow, or maybe it is time to cut one of the group's mavericks or hangers-on. Either way, it is time to get tough—without taking off the kid gloves. Sarah stands up and leaves her carrel in the Regenstein Library to go down to the machines in the basement to get some ersatz coffee.

On the way, she will touch base with each member of the group. They are all here, but no longer study together. She first walks past John's empty chair. He is the biggest problem. She knows this. She gets individuals, and how they work in groups, having used this to become the most popular girl in high school and to make things run more smoothly for everyone. She'll confirm her ability—or not—when she tests her talents on the smart and somewhat gloomy set of friends she has come to love.

As Sarah rests her hands on the back of John's chair and looks at his physics homework, she realizes she will never comprehend all that he does. He needs no help in that way. The problem is his response to the triangle formed by him, Melissa, and Randall, which is making each of them a bit demonic. They all seem possessed by the invisible but omnipresent campus gargoyle that projects errors onto others. John is worse than the other two together: he feels the least at fault and the most wronged, and is leaving it to others to make things right while he watches and judges. This withholding has persuaded almost everyone that he is over Melissa once and for all.

Sarah circles the third floor stacks and finds Doug in the far corner. He is the strategist who can catalyze her abilities as a social maven when they are on an up cycle. Unfortunately they wore each other out by the end of the summer term, and are now taking a break during which they sustain an uneasy but relatively friendly equilibrium, like drinkers who have been on a bender and are now on the wagon.

She winces. She knows that their down cycle is hurting the group, but doesn't know what to do about it. She looks at Doug's broad shoulders and strong arms hunched over his math home-work and feels ... nothing. He probably senses that she is there and is waiting for her to go. She retraces her steps and cuts down an aisle between shelves of books in the direction where April and Alan are seated in carrels. Although they had a rough time this summer being away from each other while coping with their families' disapproval, they have now cheered each other up, and have made a pact to put their love ahead of their families' parochial views. They are serene, and seemingly untroubled by the others.

Sarah heaves a sigh of relief. They are the least likely to hold the group, but that's a group for you. Those who are less central hold steady when the center weakens. She circles the couple, who do not look up, and then goes around the central stairwell, ducking into an aisle in the stacks where Melissa is doing the same homework that John is doing. She is maturing faster than John as she negotiates the changes that are overtaking their generation.

Even so, her choices are naïve. She slept with Randall, fine. But now she is trying to break up with him without hurting anyone, which is prolonging the impasse and hurting everyone, especially John, and through him the whole group. Sarah decides to talk to Randall, and to get Doug to talk to Melissa, who has to break up with Randall as soon as possible.

Doug is disgusted with himself. "What the fuck?" he says irritably to no one in particular. Thomas takes it personally. It is 8:00 p.m. and he is sitting at the desk of Professor Monte Lloyd, the botany teacher, looking for the answer key for the midterm exam. He got the key to the office by bribing and blackmailing the janitor, who has two jobs and uses the evening one for drinking and sleeping.

"Are you with Melissa or with me?" Thomas asks edgily.

"What?" Doug asks irritably, crossing his arms carelessly.

"Do try to keep up," Greg says. He and Thomas laugh, and Thomas goes back to what he is doing while Doug tries to figure out how he got himself into this mess. Thomas had told him that he wanted to correct his answers, which isn't something Doug would do. He likes the satisfaction of winning by fair play, but it didn't especially bother or surprise him that Thomas wanted his way and didn't much care how he got it, or that Greg liked secrets and subterfuge for the same reason he liked the law—he liked getting away with whatever he could. Plus, they were all a bit high on uppers and testosterone, and inclined toward trouble, although sober enough to want that trouble to be safe.

And then it got nasty. Thomas would eat a ham sandwich on his grandmother's grave, but certain trip wires activate his Jewish roots, and one of those is a Jewish man loving a non-Jewish woman. He took vicarious pleasure in Alan's and Randall's deflowering of April and Melissa, but when he found out that "his" yids had become serious about the *shiksas*, he dusted off his Yiddish vocabulary and badmouthed them to any Jew who would listen.

But when Alan and Randall ignored Thomas, his vitriol overflowed, and now he is altering their answers to exam questions—which Greg is eager to be part of now that he has the bizarre notion that he wants to get in Melissa's pants. And because Randall is widely known as the key that opens the lock, the lover who ignites a woman's sexual passion, Greg is angry that Melissa hasn't responded to *his* licking of his lips to let her know that he's willing to go down on her.

And now Doug finds himself aiding and abetting two people for whom he has no respect, who are hurting friends he cares about in all too consequential a way.

"I gotta go," he says, turning away and thinking he needs to convince Melissa to write her homework and exams in ink—and to break up with Randall.

"What's the matter," Greg begins sarcastically.

"You know what it is," Doug parries with a snap. He goes out and leaves Greg to fill in the blank. The last thing Doug hears as the door is closing behind him is Greg saying in an all-knowing tone, "Sarah. They go at it like they're in the ring. You should hear them!"

John puts on his black wool beret. The week has been unusually cool and the night air between the Midway and 63rd Street is stiffening his fingers and lips. As he passes a vacant lot where a street light is turning a patchy layer of broken glass into a carpet of coarse glitter, he reflects on the decay of the Garfield neighborhood: It is as if the desolation has erased the material past to make way for the birth of new music that expresses longing for life.

There were forests here a little over a century ago—forests as magnificent as those he saw in Alaska—and that he longs for as much as or more than he longs for the relief that he will enjoy as soon as Melissa is his. She is right. He is a man now, one with a history. Or who knows his soul and his soul mate. He may only love like this once, and would not miss anything it has to offer. If they turn out to be as antagonistic as Doug and Sarah, so be it. But they won't. They will rocket into a future of exploration.

Leaving the university behind he approaches 63rd Street, which would have been busy in the years before the riots but is now dominated by abandoned, heavily barred storefronts. He recalls the first time he came to this part of the city to hear Muddy Waters, and then to play his harmonica—also called a harp—the pocket instrument that none of the pros play. He had jammed with the musicians as they warmed up before the first set, and they humored him kindly at first, but when they saw that he could hold his own, they invited him to play along during the middle of the performance on Thursday nights. For them, it was a diversion, but for John it was a dream come true. And, in addition to being the first taste he'd had of adult respect outside of the classroom, every once in a while he even earned a tip.

The bouncer recognizes John and lets him in without interrupting his conversation with a wino who is sitting on the pavement drinking from a bottle hidden in a paper sack. The saxophonist is already here, warming his fingers and his embouchure, and John grins as he warms up while circling the tables and approaching the stage. Because the tech is blinding them with spot checks, it takes John a moment to realize that the owner is motioning for him to come into his office.

John pockets his harmonica and walks around the stage as he follows the owner to the inside door that had, until now, been closed to him. He feels more and more uneasy as he enters the modest and cluttered office dominated by autographed photographs of some of the most accomplished musicians of the day. John hopes that he will be offered a job, but can tell from the owner's demeanor that something may be wrong.

"John, there's something I have to talk with you about. It's your playing with the band. I have to be straight with you. I've had some complaints. Some of the white folks that come down here don't like seeing a white musician playing the club, especially a kid."

John is momentarily disoriented. That is the last thing he expected to hear. The owner goes on.

"Now John, my business depends on these people and what they say to their friends. They come a long way out of their neighborhood over to my club to hear black music. When they see a young white boy up there, they feel like they're not getting what they come for. Some of them probably don't know the first thing about music, but they're my customers, and I got to give them what they want."

John had often noticed groups of reserved, goggle-eyed white spectators. They seemed to him to represent the voyeurism of many whites who visited black neighborhoods on the south side, and who were more respectful than the white men who drove in from near and far to try out black whores beyond the reach of their families' and neighbors' imaginations. He recognizes their objections to him as a nuance of Jim Crow that he can not escape.

The owner goes on to say many kind things, that for the musicians it is about the music, that they had all enjoyed having him, but that they have to protect the business, and so on. John knows that his playing has been a casual arrangement, and that the owner is being kind and understanding, but takes the news hard.

Usually when he leaves The Hive, his head is full of musical ideas, but tonight, he is acutely aware of the ugliness that surrounds him. He notices the sticky pull of the sidewalks where drinks were spilled, the flattened fast food debris, and the smell of garbage. He loses his appetite. He feels the fixed stares, stone faces, and belligerent stances of other men at the bus stop and turns north at the first chance—as if to run from misery and defeat.

He tries to shake a feeling of foreboding, but cannot quite do it. Feeling an impulse to seek out a friend, he can't think of one who is not currently struggling with the blues, and his heart begins to ache. Taking out his harmonica, he eases his disappointment by playing a few riffs that he has been working on, realizing that he can at least play them for his own pleasure—and is gratified at the nods he receives from men he passes on stoops and curbs.

He is feeling relieved but troubled by the time he reaches 53rd Street and enters Beaulieu's Café. He grabs a coffee and a slice of pecan pie, chats briefly with Miss Taylor, and sits at his usual table. Jerome may, if he is not busy, come over to sit with John and talk. He has sought Jerome's advice about women, and Jerome has shared stories about his girlfriend Livonia and his brother Valiant, known as Val, whom John now recognizes as the rangy man who was there the night of the shooting, and who sold Thomas something, presumably pills lifted from the hospital where he works.

Just as John is ready to give up and go, Jerome comes over, says hello genially, and sits down with a cup of coffee as if expecting a long conversation. "You look low, little brother."

John feels self-conscious. "I was at The Hive tonight, and it got me down, I guess."

Jerome shows his surprise. "You been down to the Hive? What took you down there on a Tuesday?"

"Muddy Waters. I've been jamming with him for months. But when I went to play with his band tonight, the owner turned me away."

Jerome seems duly impressed. "What instrument you play?"

"Mostly blues harp and saxophone. It was race. Not the way I expected," John snorts incredulously. "Some white people complained about me being a white kid."

Jerome squeezes his eyes shut and then smiles and teases, "I'm telling you. You white people are strange." When John doesn't respond, Jerome says paternally, "Well, cheer up little brother. You must be good if you been playing with Muddy. You hang in there. You'll get another break. Besides, you can't let a little thing like that get you down. You want to be a musician; you got to do some jail time or turn to crime. You got to live the blues to play them."

John smiles now. "I've been in the Ivory Tower. Cramped, but predictable."

"You stay there. It's tough on the outside."

Jerome asks after Melissa and his other friends, and John lets on that they are all struggling. He does not expect Jerome to take this observation seriously, but his face grows solemn and he says, "It's a tough age. If things don't go just right. If there's no one there to help in the right way at the right time."

Jerome goes on to tell the story of his brother: Their father was a hard-working, strict man who could be harsh. He had worked his way up to foreman at a steel mill in South Chicago, and had high expectations. He was the kind of man they called a John Henry, one who might work himself to death proving his worth. Jerome and his brother were close, only a year apart. Jerome had always been good-natured and ready to take any opportunity that appeared; but Val had been moody, and struggled. Jerome wasn't aware of the differences between them until Val got a job, and then lost it at eighteen, became resentful, and took to the streets. Since then, his trouble and transgressions have escalated.

"We grew up in the same house, with the same advantages, but once he took a downturn, that was it. All of us, including our church community, did everything we could to help him turn things around, but nothing worked. And last fall—after that shooting—I had to ask him not to come back. Ruining my business wouldn't help him. You'd think with his jealousy and envy and malice that he'd never been to church, never learned right from wrong."

"Was he involved in the shooting?"

"I suspect so."

"I saw him selling drugs to a classmate."

"All I can do now is hope and pray and give him a little cash when I'm worried about what he might do if he doesn't get it."

"Wow. You think he would have been alright if he hadn't lost that job?"

"I think he would have got through to good times if he'd had a good employer."

John nods. "That does feel like an omen."

"Take it as a caution, little brother. Take it as a caution."

14

Party

Walking down the midway under a row of elms that reach up gracefully into the darkness, Melissa wonders how it is that Doug was able to persuade her to go to a party at Thomas' apartment. She is fairly sure that people there will be taking drugs, and may even be having meaningless sex—or worse. He told her that Sarah wasn't speaking to him, which was plausible, and that he was ashamed to go out on a Friday without a date, which is fishy. It's obvious Doug is concealing something, but is also truly distressed and wants her help, so she hopes he is now as street smart as he thinks he is and that this will not turn into another episode like the motorcycle incident. She is also concerned that nothing interfere with her planned breakup with Randall, whom she hasn't seen for two whole weeks.

As they walk west along the south edge of the Midway Plaisance, Melissa feels more and more anxious. She makes a point of avoiding the DMZ, or demilitarized zone, and now they are on the wrong side of it. As they cross a street, she looks south and sees a young white male run out of a gray six-flat carrying a huge plastic packet filled with white powder. He jumps into a waiting car filled with students, which then speeds away.

"Not too discreet," Doug says.

"Where is Thomas' place?"

Doug points out the windows of Thomas' apartment, which is ahead of them on the left in a corner brick building of modern design. The second-floor apartment has floor to ceiling windows that are brightly lit and covered only by a sheer curtain. As they approach, Melissa spies two figures through the fabric. One is Thomas, stark naked, and standing behind a nude woman facing the street. It takes Melissa a moment to believe that he is doing it to her from the back, in plain sight, or that they are passing a group of black men who have congregated across the street to watch. She stops and looks at Doug, who shrugs and says, "Thomas likes to put on a show."

"Doug! Why did you bring me here?"

"You need to see the way Randall is when he's not with you."

"Why don't you just tell me?"

"I've tried to tell you before, but you haven't wanted to listen."

"I'm listening now."

"Do you want to know?"

Melissa hesitates. Curiosity overcomes her better judgment. "Yes."

"Then let's go in." Doug pulls his hat down over his eyes and leads her into the vestibule and on up to the apartment.

"It's OK. You're with me," he says, as if to reassure himself.

When they reach the door of the apartment, Greg opens it for Doug with a smile. When he sees Melissa he scowls and opens his mouth to object.

"She's with me," Doug says firmly.

Greg backs up, saying, "She's your responsibility, then," and disappears into the apartment.

Doug and Melissa walk into a low-lit living room of modest proportions filled with the sweet, heavy smell of hashish and the sound of rock music coming from another room. A large bong and several plates of snacks sit on a square coffee table surrounded by floor pillows and a set of leather Scandinavian design furniture where eight or ten people are lounging. Polished oak flooring and framed prints glow yellow in the light of several candles. Two couples disappear quietly into a room down the hallway.

As they sit down by the low table, Melissa begins to realize that most of the others around the table are in a stupor. One of them is Randall, who draws a deep breath through the bong and leans heavily back on one of the pillows next to the table. He is there and not there. A woman is leaning over him, cupping his crotch. She sits with a look of confused hostility. It is Anne Lange, whose blouse is unbuttoned down to her bra. "I didn't realize this was your kind of party," she says sardonically.

Melissa feels sick. Randall does not seem to have noticed her. It is over. Entirely and irrevocably over. Anne moves to hand the mouthpiece of the bong to Melissa, who pushes it gently away and says, "You can have mine. Thanks."

Anne frowns. She is having trouble concentrating. Another woman takes the bong from her.

Doug takes a pot brownie, waiting for Randall to recognize them. When he does, he sits up and stares at Doug angrily, but after a minute shakes his head in disgust before saying, "Have it your way, then."

"I will," Doug says smartly, reaching for the bong.

"Angel dust?" Randall asks Melissa with a sardonic laugh.

"I thought you didn't do hard drugs," Doug said, frowning and taking off his hat.

"I changed my mind," Randall replied.

"I'll have some," Anne says, sitting up with effort. "Let's go in the back." She puts her hand on his thigh, runs it between his legs teasingly, and stands up.

Randall gets up, takes Anne's hand and pulls her down the hall, but before going out of sight grabs her, kisses her hard, and puts his hand in her open blouse. As Anne unsnaps his fly, he pulls her into a back room, and closes the door with his elbow.

Melissa tries to hold back her tears by biting the inside of her cheek as Doug tries to collect his wits. Randall's brazenly hostile behavior has taken him completely by surprise. Although Randall usually ends his relationships by making himself unavailable, he has always been discreet, and has repeatedly refused to bang Anne. Doug can't tell who played whom.

Then, just when Doug is about to suggest that they leave, a door at the end of the hall opens and Val Beaulieu comes out. As he puts an envelope in the inside pocket of his jacket, Melissa feels a moment of sheer terror until she realizes that he has not broken in. Something even more incredible is obviously true: He is a guest. Greg, who has come out of the door behind him, watches silently as Val leaves.

Melissa forgets about Randall, about Anne, about Doug. She springs and runs toward Greg to confront him in the narrow hall.

"What the hell was he doing here?"

Greg grabs her arm roughly and draws her into the bathroom. "What do you mean?"

"That was Val Beaulieu. I know about him. He's an ex-con."

"Taking care of business."

"Business?"

"He's my dealer."

"He's dangerous."

"Of course he is."

Melissa is confused. Thomas' world is inverted: Bad is good and good is bad. She is horribly out of place and glad of it.

"I'll go now."

"Best decision you've made all night."

"I agree."

Melissa runs out the door, down the stairs, and all the way outside and across the DMZ. She has no idea where Val has gone, but feels safer outside than she did inside. Try as she might not to think of Anne feeling up Randall, and vice versa, she cannot get it out of her head.

Randall, who has heard Melissa confront Greg and then run out, is sober enough now to feel shame and regret. He should not have hurt Melissa, and now he is going to have to hurt Anne. He pulls her to her feet, takes her face in his hands and says, "I have to go. I'm sorry."

Anne's frustration turns to rage, but fortunately she is too stoned to actually do anything about it, and after gently leading her to the bed Randall runs out too.

Doug is just getting a pleasant buzz from the bong as Melissa runs out of the apartment, followed by Randall. Doug is about to follow Randall when Thomas comes bursting out of the front bedroom, shouting, "Narcs! Quick! Flush everything!"

Seeing flashes of blue light through the wall of windows in Thomas' bedroom, Doug realizes that someone must have called the police.

"City or university?" Greg asks before running to the front window to look. "University," he says, answering his own question. "Thank God. They'll give us time."

The torpor ends, and the guests are all in motion. The naked woman dresses hurriedly as others open windows and turn on a fan. Those who are sober enough flush all evidence of drugs and sex. Doug's stomach churns. His mouth tastes sour as he runs desperately through the apartment looking for anything the others might have missed, but everything is gone by the time they hear the knock on the front door.

The police enter to find a sedate group of students whose faces show fear and obedience. One officer speaks quietly and calmly with Thomas while the other takes a cursory look in each room. The officers then exchange knowing glances—student parties are very low on their list of priorities—and prepare to take their leave. One turns back at the door to say to Thomas, "We're going to have to call your father this time."

Until now, Thomas has looked calm, even cocky. Now he is obviously terrified. After the officers go, Thomas paces up and down like a panther in a cage, palms pressed to his forehead.

Doug does his best to calm him. "It's better than being arrested and kept downtown. That's a great place to get butt-fucked."

Thomas looks at Doug with wild eyes. "Believe me, it would be better to be in jail."

"Surely he wouldn't hurt you."

"You don't know him."

Melissa stops at Sarah's house to tell her everything about the party and to ask for comfort. But to her surprise Sarah is angry with *her*, and with Doug—and even angrier with Randall. She all but pushes Melissa out the door so she can go right over to John's place to tell him that it was messy, but is finally over.

At first Melissa is baffled and downcast, but then catches Sarah's worry and begins to fear for John's wellbeing. Forgetting all about her own open wounds and the shocks of the evening, fearful that somehow Sarah is right and she herself is the one who is responsible for the strains that are pulling apart their dear group, she rushes to John's apartment to tell him that she is finally free.

As John buzzes her into his building, she sees Doug about a block away, heading toward their apartment by another route. Has he already been there, and perhaps even set things right? Missy takes the stairs two at a time and meets John at the door. As she moves forward to embrace him, he turns and goes into the brightly lit empty dining room, where he sits down with his arms folded and stares at her.

"Do you mind my coming so late?" she asks uncertainly.

He shakes his head.

"Things didn't end the way I wanted. I had a friendly ending all planned for Sunday, but I'm finally free, and I'm so glad—but you don't seem glad."

"I heard about your party! I'm surprised you have the nerve to come to me right after he dumped you, like you can count on my faith in you whenever things don't go your way."

"I can't believe you just said that after all the trouble we both went to."

"The Missy I know and loved would never have gone to that party. I don't know who you are."

"I'm a woman who tries to do what's right, not a woman who tries to appear to do it."

"You sound like a woman who thinks she's the only one who knows what's right."

"I'm the only one who can know and keep my conscience, which is free of that mess at the party, by the way."

John shakes his head. He looks glum, dour even. Perhaps

Sarah is right. Perhaps he needs help. But he doesn't want it from the woman he says he loved.

"You seem like a man who has judged me."

"Maybe I am."

She wants to talk back. To tell him she is disappointed. To say she overestimated him. To slap him. To embrace him. But he is far away. He is closed. She goes out not knowing what has happened, and whether her love meant anything to him after all.

15

Assault

A few weeks later, at the end of what has been a long day for each young woman, Melissa and Sarah sit in Melissa's room drinking cheap tea from chipped cups. Feeling like nineteenth century English ladies upholding the social standards of a small town, they seize on hints and innuendos offered by other students; spin cotton candy tales of tragedy, triumph, and scandal; analyze, rationalize, censure, and forgive transgressions they construe. They impose simplicity or complexity until they feel ready to meet real problems with a sense of normalcy—or delight.

They are, in short, fooling themselves. They are rationalizing what is, rather than learning to take action to alter it. They discover this the hard way as they sense the unresolved wounds and unarticulated questions that linger in their hearts.

"Who needs men, anyway?" Melissa asks in mock frustration that fails to conceal deep-seated angst.

"I'm through with men!"

"I don't look to any man for guidance. I just do all the homework they give me."

"You're a terrible feminist!" Sarah laughs. "We should take back the night *and* the day."

"I'll drink to that."

They clink teacups together and take sips of bitter brew. As their banter tends toward the sardonic, their efforts to make it relaxed and funny begin to feel forced. The underlying unease that Sarah has been sensing is becoming more rather than less intense. She has been blaming it on Doug, and on her inability to walk away from him for good, but cannot avoid the nagging notion that there are more pervasive forces at work. Perhaps it is the troubles that immerse them, the university, or the neighborhood. She turns the conversation to a dark topic that they have been avoiding in their efforts to lighten the mood.

"How about Thomas?" she asks seriously but tentatively, not wanting to bring it up if Melissa is not up for it.

"What is the matter with him? He likes to torment people!"

Thomas and Greg lost interest in Melissa when, as Greg told Sarah, Randall "gave her what she deserved." And now they are devising ways to give April what she, in their minds, deserves—and to make Alan "see her for what she is."

But Sarah can't really tell what they mean by that, except that they seem to punish anyone who violates their will. They are, perhaps, the inverse of Melissa, who refines her will and imposes it on herself. This might have made for an interesting discussion of attitude and character, but it has become malicious, and therefore disturbing, and is now a source of anxiety.

"Thomas makes no sense to me," Melissa says. "His Judaism has no ethics. He's just as mean to religious Jews as he is to gentiles."

"He went too far when he tormented April and Alan at the library the night before exams. Alan isn't doing that well and Thomas knows it, and April's parents are pressuring her to transfer to a small college in Iowa, and he knows that, too."

"He conned Doug into gossiping and used all his juicy little tidbits to stick in the knives and twist them."

"He knows how to psych them out and make it look like it's their fault for being vulnerable."

"What did he say to Alan? You must have heard."

"I was sitting nearby, but was focused on my homework and didn't hear them until he started asking all these physics questions that Alan couldn't answer, and saying they were going to be on the test. Small things, but perfectly calculated to unnerve Alan."

"Why *is* Thomas taking physics?"

"He wants to be a doctor, and thinks the whole world is against it."

"I am. For all the good that does," Melissa says.

Sarah sighs. "He did the same thing to April, calling her a *shiksa*, saying how Alan's parents will hate her and cut him off and pretend that he's dead if he continues to pursue her."

They sip tea silently for several minutes. Grades and religion are sensitive topics, but with Thomas having violated many taboos with impunity, they are unable to come up with a way to address it all except by psychoanalyzing him, and then sharing their conclusions with April and Alan. They are comforted by the idea that he is, deep down, trying to get back at his father or his mother, which is an impulse that almost every student has felt and can accept as an explanation for the unacceptable.

While Sarah is pressing the last drops of lemon juice from a wedge, John bursts into the room, his face gripped by a wild look. Melissa looks away. They have not spoken since the night of the party.

"What's the matter?" Sarah asks.

"Get your coats," John says, his voice tense and portentous.

Melissa steals a glance at his face, which wears the same

expression it did when he ran away after their first fall lunch at the Blue Gargoyle. Doug is standing behind John, looking unhinged. She and Sarah exchange worried looks. They grab their coats and put them on while running down the stairs after the guys, who are already heading south toward the campus.

Sarah's head is filling with scattered fears that coalesce into a hard knot when John slows down enough to tell them that several minutes earlier, while walking home from the library, he spotted Alan in a police squad car parked at the curb—but just as he went over to the car, it pulled away.

Alan, whose face apppeared to be scraped up badly, had rolled down the window and shouted, "Get Melissa and meet me in the Emergency Room."

When they start to run again, Doug realizes that even though he has been expecting trouble since orientation day, he has no idea what to do now that it has come to them. The only thing he can think to do is to run faster. When they arrive at the Emergency Room, panting with fear and fatigue, he feels angry that they have to stand there as if their world is not coming undone, and must obey the impassive clerk who waves them callously into an adjacent waiting area.

John looks numbly at the sea of bright blue plastic seats in the waiting area, most of which are filled with strangers whose faces are set to blank. When Melissa and Sarah take two empty seats at the back, Melissa tries to look invisible. John and Doug, who decide to stand nearby, can't help but pace and fidget with worry as they wait for what seems to be hours. Gradually, they, too, look blank.

The outer glass doors whoosh open to admit a tall, thin man in a ski hat whose café au lait face is covered with mahogany moles.

Cursing—and at times pushing—invisible enemies, he lurches around the banks of seats, and gestures wildly at empty air. People come to life: A well-groomed policeman at the door shifts his right hand to the handle of his club. A large woman fans herself with a folded newspaper while calling on Jesus. A young man in the far corner, who is wearing a shower cap over his Wet Look hair treatment, opens a switchblade to impress a slip of a girl in the next seat.

The hallucinating man takes a seat between two large women, and as he slowly grows calmer the room regains its torpor. After an indefinite time, Livonia, the charge nurse, emerges from the inner doors. Melissa and John know her as Jerome's girlfriend, but Doug and Sarah see her only as a strikingly beautiful woman with a heart shaped face, large Afro, and preoccupied expression. As she takes a chart from the receptionist, John calls out, "Livonia!"

Livonia looks up at John with one eyebrow raised. She nods gravely. John approaches her and Melissa follows. Livonia says in a low voice, "Hello, kids." Livonia is crosstalking, but says the last word familiarly as key-ids.

"Your friend's inside. She's doing okay. Alan is here, too. You two have volunteered here, so you can go back to your friends if you want to."

"We do!" Melissa replies fervently while John nods in agreement.

"Follow me," Livonia says to Melissa. "John, I'll point you to the boy."

Livonia opens the inner door, gestures down a hallway to the blood donation room, and nods to John who quickly disappears into the room.

Melissa, who is less sophisticated than Livonia knows, follows numbly through a foyer cluttered with wheelchairs and crash carts and on down the hall to the left, where the row of curtained alcoves smells of rubbing alcohol, antiseptic, and urine.

Acutely aware of patients, visitors, and beeping machines, and the crash suite where the trash baskets are heaped with bloody papers, Melissa soon hears the kindly voice of Dr. Stein, whom she once shadowed in the role of unofficial volunteer. Livonia signals for her to wait in a chair and disappears. Within moments, she reappears with Dr. Stein, whose curly black hair and full beard are spread out in mad-scientist fashion. The two go behind the curtain, which billows outward for a few long seconds as they begin to speak in low tones. As April replies in a high, tearful voice, Melissa is able to gather that she has been raped, that the wall between her vagina and rectum was torn, and that Dr. Stein will be stitching it closed with sutures.

When Melissa hears Stein's graphic questions, and April's tense replies, she digs her fingernails into her palms as she recalls Randall's tender skill, and the pain and bleeding of her broken hymen. That was bliss next to this. She hears Dr. Stein mention semen samples, and she pictures his hairy hands reaching in with a steel tool to scrape the delicate tissues beyond the cruel wound.

A circle of light appears revealing the silhouette of Dr. Stein's hair, which moves like weeds in a breeze, and of Livonia's Afro, which casts a smooth circular shadow. Melissa listens as Livonia explains to April what Dr. Stein is doing as he places a cold metal speculum into her vagina to look inside; prepares to take samples, which may cause her pain; and uses a needle to inject some numbing medicine before putting in the stitches.

Melissa presses her hand over her own pubis protectively and slips into sympathetic shock as she tries to tune out April's high, tense cries, while tuning in Livonia's low, soothing comforts. She welcomes the distraction when a man in another alcove vomits and curses. The next thing Melissa knows, Livonia is smiling tenderly and holding the curtain open. She nods, then enters the now dim alcove, trembling as she moves forward to the cart where April is lying on her side, facing the wall, her back perfectly still.

After Livonia and Dr. Stein leave, Melissa quietly says, "April, I'm here. Are you okay?"

"No," April replies in a tiny voice.

"I came with John. Alan's here somewhere, talking to the police. Sarah and Doug are in the lobby."

"This is my punishment for being with Alan."

"Oh, April, no. You were—attacked." Melissa puts her hand on April's arm. "How could it possibly be your fault?"

April pulls away. "I don't know. It just is. I don't want to talk about it."

"Okay." Melissa sits down on a chair crammed between a sink with a foot pedal and a cart overflowing with supplies. "Can I get you something? Tea?"

"I don't want anything."

Melissa feels horribly helpless. She stands, then sits down again.

"I want you to call my parents," April says in a high whisper. "Ask for my mother. Tell her what happened, and tell her to tell my father. Don't talk to him! You don't know what he's like. He'll make me go home!"

"Okay. Don't worry. I'll call." Melissa is grateful to be given a way to help. She hops up and skirts the curtain, turning back to ask, "Do you want to see Alan?"

"No."

"Can I tell him you're going be okay?"

April snorts.

Melissa heads to the door that John entered, peeks in, and sees him sitting in an armless chair staring absently at the floor. Alan, sitting on a huge green-upholstered recliner, is running his finger around the coffee cup mark on its arm. His shirt is off, and his nose and ribs have been taped.

Melissa enters and stands awkwardly inside the door, but before she can speak, two young white police officers enter and ask Alan for a statement. Melissa digs her fingernails into her palms again and goes to stand next to John, whose eyes seem to plead forgiveness. She offers it tacitly by standing by him and taking comfort in him, in the room, and in the officers who promise stability, order, aid, and predictability.

Alan rambles, and keeps repeating, "It all happened so fast." The policemen eventually piece together the story: Alan and April were walking toward Sarah's house when they passed two older black men coming the other way. Seeing that one was in a rage, April smiled to placate him. Alan was appalled. He knew not to smile, and put his arm around her, pulling her along as they quickly passed the men. Alan thought everything would be okay, but suddenly April was rising into the air and he was lying on the sidewalk.

He couldn't breathe. Blood blocked his nose, icy pavement scraped his cheek, and a man was sitting on his back. Alan heard the dull sound of fists on flesh, fabric tearing, and a man grunting as April screamed with each grunt. After that, nothing made sense.

The younger officer, looking sharply at his senior partner, says, "We already interviewed two eyewitnesses, students who saw the whole thing from their front window." The older man pats Alan's shoulder, and the officers leave.

Now that he has started, Alan can't stop talking. Melissa can't tell if he knows that she and John are there. He seems to be talking to the coffee stain about the agony of lying on the ground, of feeling a cold breeze on his back, of hearing footfalls and slamming car doors, and being too stunned to get up and go to April, or too afraid. When he starts to cry and verbally castrate himself for failing to act, Melissa puts her arm around him and says, "April thinks it's her fault and you think it's yours. Neither of you is to blame. You are both innocent." But all he can do is sigh, and clutch her arm.

John adds quietly, "Alan, you were just walking home, man. It shouldn't have happened."

Alan shakes his head. "Things will never be the same."

"Alan, hey man. Soldiers get over war. You'll get over this."

"She's never going to get over this. We'll never—" Alan starts panting as if he might panic.

As Melissa hears a sharp knock, Dr. Stein enters and puts his hand on Alan's shoulder. When Alan appears to be hyperventilating, the doctor pulls a paper bag from under the chair and tells him to breathe into it. When Alan is calm again, it is Dr. Stein's turn to ask what happened.

"I ... she ... I couldn't do anything. I was on the ground ... I heard ... there was nothing I could do."

Dr. Stein replies matter of factly, "If you'd resisted, she might be dead. Remember that. There was nothing you could do. But you can do a lot now. April's going to need a lot of T. L. C."

Alan nods absently, shakes his head, and then nods deliberately.

After Dr. Stein releases Alan from his care and leaves, Melissa says, "The doctor is finished with April. She's resting. I'm going to call her parents."

As Alan nods, Melissa puts her hand on his arm again, and he lets her comfort him for a moment before saying, "I want to see her."

"I'll take you after I call. It might take a while."

Alan nods.

John says, "I'll go with you, Missy. Okay Alan?"

Alan lets his head fall back and his eyes close. He sighs and nods.

John follows Melissa out into the lobby and into the entry vestibule where there is a pay phone. He takes her in his arms and whispers, "I'm sorry."

She holds him tight and breathes in a choppy staccato that is half laughing in relief and half crying in tragic sorrow. As he kisses the top of her head and she puts her cheek on his shoulder, he can feel her breasts resting beneath his pecs on his lower ribs—but pulls away before his penis engorges. Taking her hands in his, he rests his forehead against hers.

"That was our first hug," she whispers.

Before he can reply, Sarah, who has just returned, says, "You can do that later. What happened?"

Doug works his fists as John and Melissa let go of each other and turn to look at Sarah. Melissa holds John's hand, takes a deep breath, and tells the story in a few sentences, adding, "The attack was witnessed by two students, probably from your front window."

Sarah gasps.

"Greg and Thomas?" Doug asks, guessing that Thomas' dad must have frozen his accounts, keeping Thomas from paying his suppliers—but not from selling his entire stash to Greg. His suppliers must have found out, tried to collect from Greg, and Thomas probably tried to get there first.

"I don't know," Melissa says. "Let's not jump to conclusions."

Doug clenches his jaw and punches his palm with his fist. He'd never developed the habit of using his strength because he was big enough that he never had to. But as he has kept it up by working out in his room, he now considers smashing Thomas and Greg with one of his weights.

Then, as John notices Doug's fury and looks at him with a raised eyebrow, Doug does his best to calm down.

At this point Sarah takes the receiver from Melissa's hand, and says Melissa has done enough. Since Sarah is going nuts doing nothing, she says confidently, "I'll call. I met them when they brought her back from winter break."

John reaches for the phone and grabs it, but Sarah hangs on tight and they enter into a tug of war. When Melissa looks at Doug incredulously, he inhales deeply and smirks, which makes it possible for him to relax a little.

Finally, John says to Sarah, "Alan told me you got into an argument with them. I should do it."

Suddenly, and surprisingly, Melissa yanks the receiver from their hands and raises her voice. "When are you clowns going to realize that *I'm* the steady one?"

The thwack of her words hits John like a slap and Sarah like a scolding. They turn to stare at Melissa, mouths agape.

"Now get lost! All of you!"

Doug winks, and the three of them retreat to the lobby, where they release their tension with quiet laughter at Melissa's outburst.

16

Guilt

Doug feels as if his world is growing more and more claustro-phobic and confusing. As he walks home from the library one night after midterms, he feels like a porcupine ready to throw quills. Seeing a shadow in the bushes he walks toward it, arms spread. He knows can't stand up to a gun, but he's spoiling for a fight and could wrest a knife from anyone. When the shadows reveal only empty darkness, he swings his backpack in frustration.

He is finding it harder and harder to pull April and Alan back from the brink. Yesterday she stood in the middle of the kitchen at dinnertime and sobbed to Melissa that the rapist injected her insides with corrosive hatred, and it was burning like battery acid. *What in hell am I supposed to do about that?* At least he heard this from the safety of the hall so he could ditch dinner at home in favor of eating candy bars in the basement of the library.

Doug is disgusted with April for her lack of fight, livid with her parents for blaming her, disgusted with the university for treating her rape like a dirty secret, and aggravated with Melissa for smothering April with hugs and sympathy that offend her fussy pride. He is fed up with Alan too, who is afraid to leave before the end of spring term. Thank heaven for Sarah, who turns April's anger outward, and for Anne, who dulls April's pain with wine.

April is with Sarah now, which means he might finally get

some home time without the gloomy roommates. He can't wait. He's overdue. If he doesn't get privacy soon, he'll have to hole up in his parents' basement, where he can make his mom happy just by eating dinner.

Doug stops on the street outside the apartment, looks up, and seeing that the windows are dark, runs quickly up the squeaky stairs. But as he unlocks the dead bolts in the pockmarked door, and rushes in to enjoy some solitude, the streetlight filtering in the bay window illuminates someone lying on the sofa. *Fuck!*

After locking the door and switching on the hall light, he tiptoes into the living room and finds April, who is lying very still. Worried, he creeps close enough to hear a low groan. He curses again, then plops down on the legless armchair opposite the sofa. Sarah—or Anne—must have given April too much. He sighs, switches on the pole lamp, and as he picks up a newspaper from the floor asks in a whisper, "You okay?"

After a short time, April finally replies in a small voice, "No."

Doug puts down the paper and leans forward. "What's wrong?"

"I'm tired of living in sin."

He bites his tongue to keep from cursing, and when she begins to cry he relents, as always, and sits down beside her.

"Alan's never going to stand up to his parents."

Doug can hear Sarah's rage against the machine in April's words. She has been prim, soft, and pretty, and he is sorry to see her sour on life. He reaches forward impulsively, takes her hands, and bends over her.

"It just seems that way because you're drunk."

"You're stronger, aren't you?" April says as she looks at him with flush-cheeked adoration. Reaching up, she puts her arms around his neck and her wet lips brush his ear.

Doug keeps his cool, which is not easy since he often thinks of her when he's jerking off. He likes her narrow oval face, long dark hair, delicate neck, and narrow waist—and is wild about the way she looks when she lies down in the study pit at Harper Library, hair curled around her breasts.

But she is his roommate, and is Alan's girlfriend, so he removes her arms and takes her hands again. "Alan's okay, he's just—like a matzoh ball without the soup. It's tough for him, too."

Just then the door opens, and Doug looks up to see Alan standing in the dark hall, gaping at them. Suddenly Alan runs at Doug, hooks an elbow around his neck, and pulls. As Doug tips backward, he knocks over a side table, which collapses with a crash. When Doug hits the floor, Alan sits on his belly and tries to pummel him, but Doug raises his beefy arms and pins Alan to the floor like a bug.

Alan struggles helplessly. "What were you doing to April?"

"What was I doing? She made a pass at me, you schmuck."

"She would never make a pass at you!"

"Oh yeah? Like you would never tell me that you might back out?"

Alan goes limp. "I was just blowing off steam."

"Well, blow it at each other and leave me out of it!" Doug's voice is firm as he stands up and backs away.

As Alan gets up and backs onto the edge of the armchair, he asks April bitterly, "Why Doug?"

After clumsily lifting the end table, and then falling back on the sofa, April answers quietly. "He's nice, and he's strong."

"You get stinking drunk and make a fool out of me, and tell me I'm weak for not liking it?"

Doug knows he should leave, but he has been waiting for an explosion for weeks, and doesn't want to miss it.

"I want to go, or I want out. You say you care but we're still here."

"You can't blame me!" Alan screams as he jumps to his feet. "There was nothing I could do!"

Doug and April look at each other, and then both stare at Alan in surprise. Doug says, "You think it was your fault?"

"Of course I don't blame you. I blame me!" April says.

"You blame me, I know you do. Everyone does. It's not fair!"

April goes to the armchair and puts her arms around Alan. She is standing over him, bending over awkwardly. They are both crying. "We'll go right after finals," Alan says.

Doug slinks out and heads for John's place.

A week later, when Doug feels that he can leave his roommates alone at night, he goes up the sinking stairs of Sarah's front stoop and for the hundredth time thinks that the house isn't half bad for a student slum. Peeling off his winter wear as he passes through the entry, he throws it on the floor. He's in no mood to be house tame.

He goes up the stairs and knocks as he pushes into Greg's room, where Doug finds Greg standing in surprise in his underwear. His look of fear and remorse tell Doug everything he needs to know, but he wants to be sure he has all the facts.

"Spill."

"It wasn't our fault," Greg says hopping on one foot and sticking the other in the jeans that he has picked up from the floor beside his double bed. Doug assumes Greg had been hoping to get a woman into bed—or maybe Thomas—and that hope never dies.

"It was bad timing, bad luck."

"You saw the whole thing?"

Greg nods as he pulls his T-shirt from a pile of dirty clothes under his desk, and gestures for Doug to sit on the dirt-streaked sheets on the unmade bed.

Instead, Doug walks to stand nose to nose with the wiry Greg, pulls the desk chair toward him and puts his boot clad left foot on it, then crosses his arms on his muscular thigh. Greg meekly takes the one-down position by sitting on the bed.

"I want the story—the *whole* story," Doug says tensely.

Greg tells it from the time of Thomas' party, after which Thomas' dad had paid a visit, put the fear of ruthless men into them, and emptied Thomas' accounts. He also put Thomas on a tight allowance and hired a man to tail him and make daily and weekly reports of his activities. Thomas was told to stay out of trouble, and to be in the library when he was not in class. No sex, no drugs, no business but making good on his father's tuition money.

The problem was that Thomas owed money to some tough dealers, and although he had told them that Greg would be paying his debt, Greg didn't have the money when they came to the house to collect. There was an ugly scene, but when the other people in the house came down to see what was going on, the dealers left.

"Thomas was there."

Greg doesn't contradict him.

"Who are the dealers?" Doug asks sharply, staring Greg down.

"We want to see that they get what they deserve. They were way out of line. All they had to do was wait. We didn't know they did business like that or we never would have—"

"I'm glad you've switched teams. But. Who. Were. They. I want names, numbers, everything!"

"Ask Melissa."

"Very funny."

"She saw him at the party and asked what he was doing there. She knows him. The one who did it."

Doug gives Greg the hairy eyeball and decides that he is telling the truth. "Okay. I'll ask. In the meantime, let's keep this to ourselves."

"We—Thomas—told his dad."

"Good."

As Doug trudges back to his apartment, gloved hands deep in his coat pockets, he ponders the irony that Greg and Thomas aren't the only ones who now are slaving away over their books. They all are. The fanged monster of rage-impelled violence has sobered up every student who knows April or Alan, or any of their friends. They have all cleaned up their acts and pulled together. Anne, Randall, or Zeke—or all three—often come to the apartment to walk April and Alan wherever they want to go.

Doug can't shake the image of a sinking lifeboat. They are all relying on academics, and Doug is relying on Sarah. He loves her like he loves having a pulse, but he can't be with her. She drives him up the wall with her disregard for money and her blindness to the cost of her social dreams. But when he does see her, the sex electrifies them. They're both aroused with irritation or anger all the time—neither wants to mope—and when they're not they can borrow the passion that they feel between Melissa and John, who are finally in the habit of being in the same room at the same time. Whether they have got around to doing more he doesn't want to know. Not now.

In fact, he's lost his taste for being a smart aleck. He's been sucked into the general loss of humor, insolent or otherwise. He used to be able to joke or tease or irritate April out of a low mood, but he no longer has the heart for it. Fortunately, Alan has stepped up and become a real *mensch*—and is poised to become something of an outlaw, having made plans to take April to Arizona after the end of term. He has a cousin there with whom they can stay while they get jobs and earn residency, and then put themselves through the rest of their schooling. Whenever either of them is low they hold that dream like it's their baby and they're giving it a bottle. They seem almost happy then, and Doug can believe that they're all going to come out of this funk.

When John opens the door to Beaulieu's, he hears the familiar tinkle of the bell and nods to Miss Taylor. He goes to the back, takes a plastic tray, and pushes it slowly down the line to the dessert shelf, where he selects a bright orange wedge of sweet potato pie. Then he stops at the coffee urn to release a swirl of tangy black brew into his translucent white cup. When he gets to the till, he ribs Jerome about his late hours, and Jerome teases him back about not bringing Melissa.

John takes his usual seat by the window and wonders why he feels so comforted by this ritual, and why he hasn't reacted to the assault like the others. Melissa and the others stay in at night unless they get a large group together, but John goes half a mile out of his way to stop at Beaulieu's on his way home from the library. He tells himself he needs the exercise, but the truth is that he feels compelled to escape from the gloom of the Ivory Tower.

John dispatches his pie in a few bites, then downs his coffee in a few swigs. He stands, slings his backpack on his shoulder regretfully, and goes to the front door. When he opens it, and its bell chimes, Miss Taylor appears at his side and startles him by grabbing his arm. Pressing her forefinger to her lips with a stern frown as he stares in surprise, she motions him to sit on a chair behind the stacks of community papers by the door. John complies, then Miss Taylor turns out the front lights and returns to the sink to clean up. John sits still, his right heel bobbing up and down. Unable to see anything from where he is, he peeks around the papers and observes Jerome closing out the till in the cone of light cast by a metal pendant lamp.

Miss Taylor, who is scrubbing a pot in the sink, soon bellows: "That no good brother of yours gone done it now!"

"Now you always saying things like that about Val," Jerome replies easily.

"You don't never want to know," she scolds in her booming contralto. "But now you got to. He done gone up against the man this time."

Jerome looks up from the cash drawer, a troubled expression on his face. "Miss Taylor, if he's in some trouble, it's best I know."

"I come up the hard way Mr. Beaulieu. Can't nobody get nothing out of me, not even you. I don't want to make no trouble with those *friends* of his."

John hears the subtext behind her words. She said the word friends sarcastically, and is referring to enemies of whom she is afraid. He knows enough of the local vernacular of indirection and misdirection to deduce that Val belongs to a gang, probably the newly criminalized Blackstone Rangers, although he can't imagine why Miss Taylor would allow *him* to know that too.

"Miss Taylor, did he kill someone?"

John leans forward until he can see Miss Taylor scraping a stainless steel pan with a giant spoon. After turning the pan to let the tap water drum on it, she pushes a mop toward the kitchen door and knocks it closed.

"You know I be fi'n to tell you," she says in a stage whisper. She looks around furtively. "He done raped a white girl and beat her boyfriend. Two of them kids come in here."

John doesn't want to take her meaning. Chicago is a big city. Miss Taylor may not be talking about April and Alan. But then she looks in his direction and nods.

"A white girl?" Jerome asks anxiously as John feels a chill spread through the room, filling every empty chair with terror. Every black man, woman, and child on the South Side knows stories in which black men are accused of raping white women. They all end in torture and death.

"A regular customer? No. Huh-uhh. Now, why would he go and do a thing like that?"

"He ain't no good, that why. He can't stand the better man."

"But he depends on me, on my business. You know what I'm saying."

"If you got something, he take it. If he can't, he spoil it. After he come back from Joliet, they be a shooting here, and now they be a rape. The Chicago or either the university police are going to be up in here asking questions, and when they get done ain't nobody going to eat here no more."

Miss Taylor sweeps her mop like a pendulum, moving it quickly in the direction of the front door. When she reaches John she opens it and, after fixing his eyes with an intense stare, looks away and tips her head for him to leave.

John walks to Melissa's alone in the dark, his books straining the backpack which is cutting into his shoulders. For the first time he feels the weight of a dark secret that is not his own, and decides that Miss Taylor is testing his ability to keep it. After years of learning in which the ultimate purpose is testing, he assumes that she is testing him to decide whether to include him in the circle of people who look out for Jerome—but doesn't consider another possibility, which is that she might see him as an outsider who could protect Jerome by tipping off the police in order to get Val off the streets.

Doug arrives at the apartment just as John unlocks the door to the ground floor entry, enters with him, and while checking his mailbox says, "Greg claims Melissa knows the rapist."

John nods shortly.

"What the hell?"

"I do too. And so do you—well, you've seen him."

Doug holds out his hands, mouth open in mute inquiry. Though they are in the small entry, with locked doors on either side of them, John moves close to Doug and whispers, "Sarah thinks you can't keep a secret."

"That's rich, coming from Miss Motor Mouth."

"Can you?"

"If I have to. Do I have to?"

"Yes. We need a strategy."

"I'm all for that."

John explains what he has just learned at Beaulieu's. Doug whistles softly.

"And you want to keep Jerome out of it."

"Absolutely."

"And we want to keep Greg and Thomas out of it."

"We do?"

"You can call in an anonymous tip—or we can have Zeke or Anne call it in—but we may need Thomas' dad."

"Why?"

"This is Chicago. Nice people aren't the ones who get things done."

"I know you're right. But I don't want to know it. And I don't want to know it was Val."

Doug smiles for the first time that day.

"I know what you mean, buddy boy, I know what you mean."

17

Rescue

Sarah tries to comfort the boy who is laying on a gurney in one of the Billings Hospital Emergency Room alcoves. Despondently facing the wall, he is an ordinary freshman—slender, lithe, and nothing like Doug, who is unusual for his bulk.

When the boy asks in a tiny, fractured voice "Why me?" Sarah guesses he is worried about his sexuality. Ignoring what little training she has received as a volunteer rape counselor, she says with a mother bear snarl, "A perp like that doesn't know anything about anything! You were just in the wrong place at the wrong time."

The boy looks at her warily. Apparently satisfied with her confidence or contempt—or her breasts—he says with relief, "You're right! He didn't know anything about me."

"You can be sure of it! He was just looking for a target."

He heaves a deep sigh.

"Will you be alright now?" she asks.

"Yeah. I'd like whatever privacy I can get."

"You bet. I'm so glad that it wasn't any worse," she adds, thinking of the last case.

"You've seen worse?"

"Yeah. Stitches, casts, you name it."

"That's terrible. I didn't know."

"It is terrible. And there's very little help, especially for the guys. If you're up to it, we'd love to have you as a volunteer. It can help you—and them."

As Sarah walks away, she wipes tears from her face. She has tried so many ways to get help for students who were raped, and can see now why Anne mocks her efforts. Weitzman, Henshaw, and other faculty have evaded and avoided her; others have even turned on her. She wonders how many perps there are in plain clothes, walking amongst the students, rationalizing violation. After trying to talk to students, and to anyone else who might listen, she finally made her way to a group of volunteers, most of them victims of rape themselves, who take calls and support new victims. The ultimate self-sufficiency group, it also finds lawyers and others who provide professional help.

She wants to help, to be part of the solution, but every teatime this spring she and Missy have talked about the tightrope walk between selfish complacency and burnout, and Sarah has finally burned out. She is not sure how much one person can do, but she has to admit that spending time with April and Alan and the others is already more than she can handle. Her grades are slipping, and if she tries to right every wrong she sees she'll end up a hedonist, or worse—a nihilist.

This secret of Val's guilt weighs on John until midterms, when April and Alan ask John to come to the police station to look at a lineup of suspects. John agrees immediately. He dreads seeing Val in the lineup, or worse, not seeing him and having to decide how to speak out for justice. He isn't sure which is just, making sure that Cain goes to prison, or protecting the business of Abel. And it isn't nearly as simple as he had imagined before he came to this troubled neighborhood and came face to face with the ambiguous moral choices of manhood and its unforeseen responsibilities.

On the last day of midterms, after completing his exam, John joins April and Alan for the cab ride through the gritty, humid streets to a precinct station on the other side of Washington Park.

When they reach the massive station, the three friends count their change, pay the driver, and the cab speeds away. They climb the imposing stone staircase and cross a worn marble threshold. Inside the cool lobby, they stop to let their eyes adjust to the darkness, and then approach the big front desk. John tries to be strong for them, but he, too, is quailing as a clerk leads them past a maze of wood-framed offices that fill the cavernous lobby.

In a small, stuffy room at the back, a line of people waits grimly in a row of chairs at the far wall. John takes a seat beside Alan, and they wait in silence as the portly officer calls each in turn to sit in the chair beside his gray metal desk and give a statement. As John picks at a tear in the Naugahyde, he listens to a string of tales of rape—some of which are delivered without expression, and others with hot tears. After a while, it dawns on him that they are all making statements in the same case, which means that April wasn't the first or only victim, although, as far as John can tell, she is the youngest by a decade, and the only white one.

John is heartened when one victim, a plump middle-aged woman with pleasing features and a nasal voice, rises from a chair to their right and takes the seat with an air of easy dignity. She shows no trace of fear, shame, or defeat.

"Your name?" the officer asks, his fingers poised over his typewriter.

"Mrs. Mamie Troupe."

She spells it out at the officer's request. The story of her assault is like many others, but it was she, and not the police or Thomas' dad, who snared the perpetrator. One night when she came home late after work, a man came out from behind the curtains of her bedroom window, held a knife to her throat, and forced her to stay still while he climbed on her and took what he wanted. She was terrified by his anger and threats, but when he finished he was calm and relaxed, and she felt safe enough to take a risk. While he was doing up his trousers, she told him that she'd liked it and wanted his name and telephone number. He gave them to her. "And then I called you."

"You certainly had presence of mind," the officer says, impressed.

"I did what I had to do," she replies with steady dignity.

John is awash in relief. He is beginning to believe that the weight of justice will be taken out of his young hands. He hopes fervently that Jerome will yet escape the harm that Val intended, and isn't the only one who feels better. Mrs. Troupe's boldness has changed the mood in the room, and the rest give statements that are less abject. The last, a thirty-year-old woman in a headscarf, smiles at a man in a white shirt, tie, and dark glasses whom John recognizes as Mr. Tate, who stocks Beaulieu's with Black Muslim newspapers.

After the woman finishes, the desk sergeant looks at John and asks, "Mr. Torrance?"

John shakes his head.

Running a hand over his short, kinky hair the officer sighs, and then says simply, "I guess he decided not to come."

As John realizes that the missing victim is a young man like himself, the mood in the room shifts again, and he feels an undercurrent of anger.

It is Mr. Tate, who has been clenching and unclenching his fist as he waits, who finally gives it a voice. "Under the Sharia he'd be castrated!" Alan, who has always spoken harshly of Muslims, looks at Mr. Tate with an expression of grateful connection.

When the clerk returns to take Mrs. Troupe to view the lineup, she rises regally and follows him down a back hall. The wait becomes tense again, so John is both anxious and relieved when it is time for April, Alan, and him to follow the clerk down the claustrophobic hallway into a dark, closet-like room with a huge one-way mirror.

Through the mirror John can see six men of Val's height and weight standing against a dirty beige wall. The clerk inside instructs them to look straight ahead.

April squeezes Alan's arm and says in her highest, tightest tone, "Look at number four."

When John looks, he sees that it is Val, who appears small, sullen, and defeated. John is shocked at the change, as he has been thinking of Val as a powerful man malignant enough to destroy the lives of the good people who care about him—but all he sees is a pathetic loser. As John pictures Val giving Mrs. Troupe his phone number, he wonders what life has been like for Val that a single compliment could undo him, and it occurs to him that Val has no notion of what he wants or how to get it.

Alan puts his hand over April's, and John can see vindication in their faces. He feels a painful mix of relief and sorrow as Alan and April speak to the officer, and they all file back through the waiting room and out onto the front steps.

April plops down on a stair and puts a stick of chewing gum in her mouth, then another and another until she's chewing the whole pack. She asks, "How do people stand it here?"

"The same way we do," Alan replies. "They go on."

"I don't know how they do it. I can't wait until we go west!"

On the Friday night of the last week of classes, Sarah walks to Doug's apartment with her friendship group. They have grown close by seeking sanctuary in the library, and by escaping their troubles by delving deeply into their courses. Focusing on study one day at at ime and sticking together for comfort has pushed everything else out of their minds. So far so good, but Sarah can't wait to see Alan and April drive into the sunset, or to hear that Melissa and John have moved to the studio by Beaulieu's and started to have sex. Then everything will be as it should, and they can all begin to build full lives again.

Later, after a night of slow-go study at Doug's—broken by a fast meal from Harold's Chicken Shack—they take a break before bunking down for a safety sleep-over. Melissa, who is still finishing her p-chem homework, takes a pillow and sits under the bay windows away from the group that is gathering on and around the sofa and easy chairs. Their conversation halts when they are alerted by a strangely familiar click.

Melissa jumps up and runs to her room, where she finds April sitting on the bed pointing a gun at her own face. The others converge in the doorway.

"What are you doing?" Melissa asks, calmly getting April's attention as she gently takes the gun from her hands.

"I don't know. I was just thinking about spring break, and … it looked like a toy."

"A gun!" Doug says with quiet intensity as he and John enter the bedroom. "You have a motherfucking hand gun?"

"Why do you have a gun?" John asks incredulously.

"For protection. My dad insisted." Melissa's reply is delivered in a quiet, even tone of voice.

"Doesn't he know that if you have a gun in Chicago your assailant is likely to take it from you?" Doug asks angrily.

"Calm down, middle-class city boy. Where I grew up every man in the neighborhood had guns—at least one for protection and one for hunting. The question is," Melissa says, handing John the gun and kneeling down and taking April's hands in hers, "how did you find out about it and why isn't it in the box? It was way at the back of my closet shelf under my summer clothes." Melissa catches John's eye. They both frown.

"I was looking for a sweater to borrow. I like your sweaters."

"You've never mentioned it. You were thinking about break?"

April starts to cry. "I can't face them, and I can't bring Alan. I want to go away now, but he wants to go home before we go west."

"Promise me never to go in *my* closet again."

April nods obediently, but distractedly, as if she is not all there.

"When you think about things like that tell one of us, okay? We can help you figure it out."

Alan comes out of the shower, and emerges from the bathroom with a towel around his waist. When he hears what has happened, he freaks out and has to breathe into a bag again. An hour later, when he and April are asleep in his room, the rest gather in the living room to talk through what to do.

Melissa begins by recounting what April did and said.

Sarah says, "I love all of you, and I used to think that we could handle our own problems. For me, at least, it hasn't gone all that well." She recounts her plan to hurry Melissa's breakup with Randall, and apologizes to Doug, Missy, John, Anne, and Randall. She then asks, "Does anyone have any good ideas about what to do now?"

Zeke says, "We should consider the possibility that we've done enough."

Anne snorts. "She just stuck a gun in her mouth."

Randall says, "I agree with Sarah and Zeke that we shouldn't try to handle this on our own. It's too risky."

"And too much. I'm not getting enough sleep," John says.

"I don't like where this is going," Doug says. "This could take us all down. It will if we get cocky."

Everyone turns to look at Doug.

Sarah says, "I can't believe it was you who said that, but I can't agree more."

Anne says, "Counseling hasn't done that much for me, but it's good in a crisis."

The group is still for a full minute. That's the most that any of them has heard her reveal about her problems.

Sarah says, "Thank you for saying that. I've been doing some rape counseling and I don't think that volunteers like me can handle April's case."

Randall says, "We have to take her to Student Health in the morning. They can admit her and put her on medication, maybe even arrange for her to take her finals."

Melissa says, "I'll go. I won't be able to think of anything else."

"I'll go with you," Zeke says. "I'm past the point of diminishing returns when it comes to studying. I can wait there for as long as it takes them to do the paperwork, which might take all day."

18
Reckoning

Finals are over, and Melissa is hesitating outside John's door. She has lost her basic trust of others, is close to losing faith in life and love, and now is going to appeal to the love of her life, who is actually no stronger than she is. If things go well, he will let her down eventually, as she will undoubtedly let him down too.

Putting her hand on her heart she summons her courage, but as she reaches out to knock on the door, it opens, and she sees John's dear face there, looking solemn.

"Sarah said we would always have each other, but we don't," Melissa says. She thought she was all out of tears, but when she looks at his eyes, which seem to look right into her heart, they flow again. Suddenly, she and John are embracing and then kissing and pressing their bodies together. He takes her by the hand and leads her past his bug-eyed roommates, who look like a family of prairie dogs as they stare into the hall from the dining room.

John pulls her gently into his room and they go to the bed and lie down and hold each other and kiss and talk as they so often do. This time, though, she feels like she is holding onto love and life for fear they will disappear, and taking great comfort from him as from a pit fire in a wintry wilderness. As long as he is with her she will be fine. As long as they are together she will be able to meet any challenge with heartfelt confidence in humanity despite all its flaws.

"We did the right thing, taking April to Student Health after the gun episode, didn't we? We all agreed ..." Melissa's words, muffled against John's shoulder, trail off, her comfort already starting to fold in on itself.

After a long silence, John finally speaks. "Alan said that his parents were glad she was locked up."

"They were glad? How horrible."

"He's planning to sit the mourner's Kaddish for each of them, and to treat them as dead to him."

"Good for him. He has to get away. He can forgive them and reconcile with them later, after he comes to terms with all that's happened."

"I thought the Kaddish was forever."

"Nothing human is forever. We know that now."

Throughout the next few hours, their thoughts and feelings bubble to the surface, and they break the long silences during which their breathing alternates, and their bodies complement one another.

"I was thinking at the lineup that it wouldn't have taken much for any of us to be on the other side of the glass. I didn't think April would cross over and try to be a perp," he says.

"She didn't. Giving up is the opposite of lashing out."

He sighs deeply. "I hope I never understand it that way."

"Me too. I hope I never lose my fight against death of the soul."

"Let's swear to help each other keep our fight for life—if it ever comes to that."

Melissa grips him tightly. "I swear on my life to protect your life."

"I swear the same."

Sometime later they go to the kitchen, raid the fridge, and return. Melissa looks at the circles under John's eyes. "Sarah used to say, no matter what happens, we'll always have each other. But now April and Alan are gone."

"You and I have each other."

"We don't."

"What do you mean?" he asks, chewing slowly.

"We haven't made love. You haven't wanted to make love to me."

"That isn't it."

"What is?"

"We were going to take our time."

"We did."

"I … uh …"

"Is it Randall?"

John looks away. "I can't think of losing my virginity to you without thinking of you losing yours to him."

"Do you want details?"

He nods and looks at his plate. He licks his fingers and takes up the breadcrumbs. Melissa can't look at him either. She looks at the bookshelves made of old boards and cinder blocks, the military surplus desk, the full mattress and pillows on an old frame with a massive headboard that he found at the Salvation Army warehouse. It is just like him: Lean and clean, a success machine with no needless clutter or expense, but with plenty of room for soul and love. She stares at the window, too, with its bright curtains and view of a brick wall, then begins to tell him in a clear voice how she felt afraid and how much it hurt and bled. After adding how gentle and kind Randall was, and how good it was that he knew what he was doing—not panicking, or blaming her when things didn't go smoothly—she pauses and waits.

As emotions flicker over John's face like a story in another language, he shakes his head, and still does not look at her.

"I never told you what April's parents said when I called them."

"No."

"Her mother got so upset that she had to tell April's father, and he said, and I quote, 'No one will want her now, not even that Jew boy. It would be better if he'd finished her off.'"

John hides his face with his hand.

"They see her as damaged goods. You know that gun my father gave me? It was to protect my virginity. If he knew about Randall, he would think of *me* as damaged goods, and assume I would never marry. When you hold back, I feel like you think of me that way."

John looks at her in tear-streaked horror.

She bites her lips.

He springs up and pulls her into an embrace. After a while he whispers, "What if I'm not as good?"

"It isn't a sport. It's an expression of feeling. Randall's sensitive and empathetic and knows how to take pleasure from giving it. You have all that in you, and you have me to explore it with."

"I don't know how."

"We love each other passionately. Follow your passion."

"Let's lie down together for a while."

"Naked."

That day, and the days following, they become one body, one heart, one mind, and one purpose.

Epilogue

Two years later, Sarah and Melissa are having tea in the apartment that she shares with John, talking and waiting for the dough to rise so they can make pizza for their weekly gathering of friends.

The friendship group, which expanded and contracted over time with the addition of new friends and partners, and the absence of those who were away or busy, may be getting together tonight for the last time. Only Sarah and Doug and Melissa and John will gather, the rest having left immediately after graduation.

"I have something to tell you," Melissa says with trepidation. She does not want to cry, and wishes the group could remain intact.

"You're pregnant?"

Melissa laughs. "No, thank God. I'll be going to Oregon next week, and John will be staying here."

"For vacation?"

"No. He's decided to stay here for med school, so I'll be going to Oregon alone."

"After you both got in against all odds? Why?"

"His advisor got to him. UC was ranked fifth this year, way above Oregon. A spot opened up here and he feels like it would be irresponsible to turn it down."

"I can't believe it. You two seem so happy—you're our model couple. Doug and I always talk about how to be more like you."

"That's part of our problem—not you, John's desire for approval, and personal success. He wants to get ahead of the next guy, and the next and the next. And me. He wants to win the relationship."

"But he's the best at so many things."

"He agrees with you, and it's important to him that we all think so. I like it when he's on top, but I don't want to spend the rest of my life on the bottom, catering to his ego."

"That's…wow, I don't recognize you in that. Are you sure?"

"I suppose I'll eventually be able to say we had incompatible career objectives, or irreconcilable differences—something like that. But now it's breaking my heart to see him change. He always seemed to want to be his best self from his core, but now he wants to be the self that's most rewarded by the men who dole out success."

Melissa starts to cry and then laughs at herself, saying, "This is what I don't want to do—hold some kind of couple's funeral tonight." She gets up and runs to the bathroom to rinse her face in cold water.

When she returns, her face set in a rueful but tear-free smile, Sarah asks, "Are you breaking up with him?"

"No. I'm willing to stay true in the hope that he will, which will mean a long distance relationship and the chance to do what I wanted to do with Randall."

"Which was what?"

"To let the relationship end amicably."

"That's a ticket to pining for him. And making sure you lose. You should make a clean break."

"You're probably right, but I want to focus on my studies anyway, and he seems to think things will work out. We're going up to see his parents next week, which will be great—I love them—and he'll be coming out to Oregon, which will give us our first chance to camp and climb together."

"That rat! He didn't say anything!"

"He's going to announce it tonight. I wanted to tell you first so you'd have a chance to see what you think, and feel."

"You're being awfully cool about it."

"They say maturity is the ability to tolerate ambiguity, and this is already maturing me," Melissa laughs darkly.

After a long pause Sarah says, "Doug is all for the win-win, except when it comes to me. He wants control. All. The. Time. Which means I have to take control. Which will mean walking out on him."

"You've been stable for years now."

"Since the rape. Since we've been with you guys. We're not so good on our own. Maybe we're really in love with you and John."

"It'll be hard leaving you two. But this is what happens whenever you leave a school. You leave love behind along with everything else."

"You take it with you, too."

"Yes. We changed each other. And that's forever."

Acknowledgments

I would like to acknowledge the University of Chicago, its faculty and staff, and its city and neighborhood for providing a rich, diverse, and powerful education during the 1970s. It was an illuminated inferno, each part revealing the others. It was a place of extremes: suffering and transcendence, intellect and emotion, abasement and exaltation, and—above all—civic heart.

A special thanks to the students of the 1960s, who arguably averted a race war while precipitating a backlash that played out like a love-in broken up by men in blue with billy clubs. A special thanks to LBJ who tried, at least, to seed a Great Society. We still have a chance.

For mentoring, deep gratitude to: Harold Haydon, Monte Lloyd, Peter Meier, Richard Mintel, Lucia Rothman-Danes, Joel Snyder, Joachim Weintraub, N.C. Yang, and the Outing Club.

Last and not least, I am grateful to the Southern Oregon team that made this book beautiful. The appearance is due to the professional competence and creativity of cover artist Bruce Bayard and book designer Chris Molé. The readability is due mainly to coach Chansonette Buck and editors Deidre Krupp, Deborah Mokma, and Ann DiSalvo.

Such writing ability as I am developing, I owe first to my father, who taught me reading and writing at a young age. I am also grateful to editor friends Eva Silverfine and Stephanie Holt for their talent and skill in verbal expression, to writing teachers Andrea Goldsmith of the Victorian Writer's Centre, and to Wendy Call of Hugo House. They kindly put up with an unusual and neurotoxic student, trusting that their wisdom would not go to waste.

Thank you also to my book development and beta readers, especially: Jan Agosti, Anna Barón, Jessica Bondy, Cynthia Bradley, Julie Clayton, Stephanie Holt, Christopher Howell, Joel Mason, Sara Myers Wade, Berta Nicol-Blades, and Dana Smaller. Special thanks to Jan, Anna, Julie, and Stephanie for their kindness in dark times.

About the Author

Beth Alderman, MD, MPH earned her AB and MD degrees from the University of Chicago and her MPH from the University of Washington. After Board Certification in Preventive Medicine and Public Health, she took a faculty position in the University of Colorado Medical School Department of Preventive Medicine, Biometrics, and Medical Informatics, where she did population-based epidemiological studies of adverse reproductive outcomes and methodological studies in clinical epidemiology. In her next faculty position at the University of Washington School of Public Health, she focused on risk factors for birth defects.

In 1996, she fell ill with the mysterious new plague and was given the provisional diagnosis "chronic fatigue syndrome". She has spent her time since studying her own case and pondering the reasons that her beloved profession failed her so completely. Fortunately, she discovered her cure, which may be of use to others suffering from one or more of the emerging epidemics affecting humans, their habitats, and life on earth.

For more about and from the author, see the following websites:

BethAldermanMD.com	*Free Information for all readers*
DoctorsOfLife.com	*For care and cure of all lives as one*
LivingFutureBooks.com	*Publishing Website*
LivingFutureCourses.com	*Educational Website with Free and advanced Courses*

Look for author's books on Amazon.com

Other Books by
Beth Alderman

Medical Phenomenology:
Chronic Ambient Poisoning

ISBN: 978-1-7332849-2-9

One day in December of 1996, the author (a physician, medical detective, and academic epidemiologist) developed disabling brain fog following on a decade-long descent into a painful, pervasive, and unprecedented chronic illness. Having done population-based studies to research the causes of birth defects, and having thus encountered the limitations of modern methods, she had inadvertently prepared to investigate the causes of her illness—which was given the provisional and uninformative label of "chronic fatigue."

The author began a delineation of the natural history of her condition using the methods of: doctors Hippocrates, Maimonides and Oliver Sacks; the "radical empiricism" used by Dr. William James; and the phenomenology introduced by Teilhard de Chardin and Merleau-Ponty. After a fifteen-year search, she found a doctor of integrative medicine whose elimination diet relieved her brain fog, which enabled her to complete a self-study and to construct an actionable new diagnosis: chronic ambient poisoning. Unseen by doctors and obscured by medical dogma and a myriad of false diagnoses, chronic ambient poisoning defies late modern, fragmented, accuracy-challenged medical research methods and delivery systems. It also reveals that human-caused habitat injuries that afflict birds, bees, and other species are affecting humans while driving evolved life toward extinction in the way of an asteroid strike. To ignore this diagnosis is to ignore the dangers to all lives posed by maladaptive modern lifeways.

The Evolve Fertility Series

BOOK 1
Melissa's Match: *Great Society*

ISBN: 978-1-7321110-1-1

It's the early 1970s. Melissa and her friends begin their first year of college in the inner city of Chicago at a time when post-assassination riots, Great Society scholarship programs, and veterans returning from Vietnam create a sometimes explosive confluence of urban and rural, rich and poor, white and black, educated and uneducated. Coming of age in a violent, unjust, and yet hopeful time, they struggle to reconcile their hopes and opportunities with the shadows of war and the destructive clashes of senescing and emerging systems of care and cure of life on earth.

BOOK 2
Connie's Conception: *Awareness of Peril*

ISBN: 978-1-7321110-0-4

It's the late 1980s, and Connie Martin, a doctor working for the Epidemiology Intelligence Service of the CDC, is called to Colorado to investigate an alarming outbreak of birth defects. Born illegitimate in the San Luis Valley as Consuela Martín, a name known only to close friends and to her beloved gamer and programmer husband, she arrives as an unknown. Joined by environmental activists who suspect the state's Superfund sites and by doctors and parents who fear for its children, Connie attempts to discover the link between habitat destruction and damage to innocents.

BOOK 3
Melissa's Malady: *End of Modernity*
ISBN: 978-1-7321110-2-8

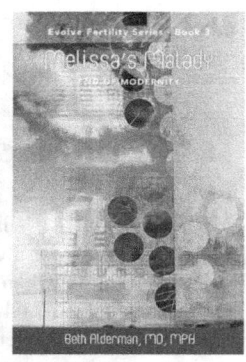

IIt is almost the year of the millennium, and Melissa meets her college friends Sarah and Doug and her first and only true love John for a reunion in Hyde Park. All four are in the midst of their careers. All struggle with the compromises that have marred their happiness. All wish to change the world, each in a different way. Sarah has left her government job for a new life as a yoga teacher. Doug is helping to birth a new value-based economy. John is a successful academic doctor. Melissa is ailing. They unite to turn John's success as a researcher to the cure of Melissa's mysterious chronic illness. What they find will change their lives and their imperiled world.

BOOK 4
Colette's Creativity: *Sacred and Profane*
ISBN: 978-1-7321110-3-5

Colette, Melissa's childhood friend, abandons her marriage and home in Maine and flies to Melbourne. There she is taken in by her friend Reggie, who seems to know the secret of joy. Colette joins in the lives of striking individuals who lead her to view sexuality as a manifestation of the sacred. As she leaves behind the wounds caused by profane sexuality, she and her new friends clash with members of Reggie's family who force them to flee and to begin again.

BOOK 5
Colette's Community: *Thirds*
ISBN: 978-1-7321110-4-2

Soon after Colette and her friends find a new home, an old boyfriend of Melissa's who is sojourning in Australia calls and expresses his desire to visit. Colette plans to use the visit as a chance to develop a job for herself; he plans to check up on Colette for Melissa. As they get to know each other, they see that despite differences in religion, origin, and experience, they are on very similar spiritual paths. When it is time for Randall to go home, Colette joins him in Chicago. When he becomes caught up in his old life, however, she returns to Australia to pursue her dream of giving birth to a sacred community.

Chronic Illness Owner's Manuals

Regenerate Your Life: Chronic Illness as a Springboard for Creating Your Best Life

ISBN: 978-1-7321110-8-0 (VOL. 1)

ISBN: 978-1-7321110-9-7 (VOL. 2)

The *Chronic Illness Owner's Manual* series is for patients with chronic illness, and for the people who care for them. Suitable for individual or small group use, it offers a comprehensive, systematic, step-by-step approach to engaging modern medical systems, and to healing from the inside out.

The books comprise anecdotes, exercises, and quotes that address recovery through seven aspects of the body: awareness, understanding, perceptions, sensations, energy, flesh, and interbeing. The frames, constructs, patterns, and processes employed by the series are drawn from traditions of medicine, field biology, theology, and psychology from around the globe. Their synthesis offers an emerging, sustainable, eco-centric, eco-contextual, and customizable approach to creating a new and better life that regenerates your unique meaning, purpose, and vision of abundant life. The *Chronic Illness Owner's Manual* series complements care and cure courses available online at www. LivingFutureCourses.com.

The Evolve Restoration Series
Sequel to the Evolve Fertility Series

BOOK 1
Pilgrim Minds: *After the War on Life*
ISBN: 978-1-7321110-5-9

Melissa's deathbed request catapults her son Aaron on a journey from her family's Mississippian clinic to the Salish Sea to claim a mysterious legacy. Meeting his niece Rafa en route, he continues overland with her, and uncle and niece come to know and depend on each other. On arriving at the Saltspring Island Research Center (SIRC), Sarah, now the keeper of the center's narratives, confesses that Aaron's legacy is a task: to apply his mother's philosophy to SIRC's lifeways in order to revitalize it.

While he had been immersed in his mother's medical philosophy, SIRC had used many of her ideas to found a fertility school. SIRC's encroaching apathy persuaded Sarah that they missed one or more essential lifeways, and hopes that Aaron may be able to pinpoint and provide them. Taken by surprise, but ready to step up, Aaron immerses himself in the community, and Rafa undergoes SIRC's initiation process. Uncle and niece come to love Cascadia and to relish local, burgeoning patterns of innovation. Both choose to stay at SIRC, an agentic community that is doing much to restore evolution and its living future.

BOOK 2
Aaron's Legacy: *The Body of Life*
ISBN: 978-1-7321110-6-6

Having come to know the community, Aaron receives his legacy as a series of enactments of SIRC's history. The surviving members of his mother's old friendship group—Sarah, Doug, and John—join the audience and performers in processing and adapting their shared narrative. In the intervals between enactments, Rafa undergoes initiation while Aaron explores the composer, an instrument that enables a player to evoke memories with images and to express the player's responses as sound scapes. As Aaron shares his with Rafa, Sarah and others, John shares memories of Melissa, and seems to receive a new message from her.

As the community adapts to changes in its meaning and purpose, Rafa and Aaron each finds a first consort and draws inspiration from local knowledge keepers and change agents residing at SIRC, the nearby Monastery of Origins and Endings, or in Victoria or Vancouver. Aaron's health, damaged by his travel through a poison barren, deteriorates. With his death, his consort Parvati shares their legacy in the form of patterns of action that may remove roadblocks to continuous adaptation and renewal.

BOOK 3

The Kindred's Rebirth: *Rough Seas and Far Lands*

ISBN: 978-1-7332849-3-6

A decade later in Australia, Parvati and Bj\u00f6rn give up on effecting meaningful restoration there. Dirk, while on his annual circuit of the north, arrives in Jokkmokk for the annual S\u00e1mi gathering to learn that SIRC is in crisis. Rafa, who is crossing the South Pacific on her two year global clinic circuit, hears strange news: the Fertility School, which was winding down, closed without notice. She realizes that her work, too, is drawing to a close as her clinics adapt to localism and begin to diverge.

All three travelers feel a strong homing urge and hatch a plan to converge in Scandinavia with the remnant of the SIRC community. En route, Parvati adopts a grandchild, Jacki, who helps Bj\u00f6rn to recover from a disorder of interbeing. Many new consort pairs join the kindred and revive it by helping to form a next community, SIRC-Umea, and to organize and maintain residential restoration communities in the Baltic and North Sea bioregions, and to recover from the painful loss of the original community.

BOOK 4

Jacki's Vision: *The Green Line*

ISBN: 978-1-7332849-4-3

When Jacki turns sixteen, she begins her transition to adulthood by venturing into larger worlds of knowledge and adaptation to gain skills. During her first clinic circuit in the Baltic, she finds that her coming of age is coinciding with her kindred's restiveness. As she embraces and contemplates her future, a vision takes hold of her. She proposes a Green Line restoration project in Tasmania to reconcile a time debt created by the Black Line genocide, and to prepare her for organizing bioregional restoration projects. Her kindred and their networks embrace the project, expand it, and multiply its potential effects.

As the Green Line Corps prepares to depart en masse for Tasmania, Jacki meets a young stranger, Mirek, whose experience of the world—whose very umwelt—contrasts with her own. Later, in Tasmania, she gains a consort, Izaak, and a sister friend, Lally, both of whom winnow her possible futures. Together, the many thousands of Green Line participants develop a restoration ethos and synchronize living processes for restoring habitats—with their restorers. Jacki and her new peers are among the first to return to the original SIRC campus, near which many former kindred members have settled, and to which many others are about to return.

BOOK 5

Mel's Motherhood: *A Place in the Living World*

ISBN: 978-1-7332849-5-0

Mel and JJ—children of the Three Mammas—await the advance boat from Tasmania at the Cascadian Monastery of Origins and Endings. Mel, who is pregnant, and JJ, who fared poorly while he was away, finished their initiation projects and are keen to see Jacki and to meet the new kindred members. In the course of a joyful reunion, Mel and JJ learn that Jacki and Lally are also pregnant.

As this next generation of adults chooses ways to express fertility and defines new vocations, the reconstituting kindred celebrates new human lives, integrates with local communities, and processes hitherto hidden threads of SIRC's history with the aid of DNA fathers who participate. The complex, complementary communities adapt to continuous learning via phenomenology, and to continuous adaptation of systems for care and cure of evolved life.

Meaningful Retirement: *Become a Life Care Provider*

ISBN: 978-1-7332849-0-5

Meaningful Retirement is a self-guided monthly course in four seasons that can aid people like you who are exiting modern employment or withdrawing from the modern death economy. In it you will find a toolbox for transition to a vocation of life care, and thus begin to mature into a wise elder able to lead and mentor those who follow you. These seasons include:

- **A Summer Breather**
- **A Fall for Reflection**
- **A Winter to Reclaim Your Personal Narrative**
- **A Spring for Revolutionizing Your Lifetime Learning**

As you transition to the role of provider of life care, you may choose to co-found emotionally and spiritually astute communities where you can mentor your juniors, who face the imminent and daunting task of passing through wrenching psycho-social change while arresting and reversing the accelerating human-caused Sixth Extinction. That threat to evolved life represents a unique crucible for transforming modern lifeways into ones that enable humans to choose and to restore life. Re-visioning and co-creating processes of care and cure that restore all lives as one will prepare your species to restore the planet's living lungs, its water circulation, its living shade, and its evolved resilience to unexpected planetary catastrophes. By viewing life in time though an eco-centric and eco-contextualized lens that scales from your lifetime to evolutionary time, you can begin to see your world through new eyes that reveal your place in the big picture of life on earth.

Direct learning, that is, phenomenology, is essential for restoration of a living future. This method has changed with every epoch since ancient natural historians began to attempt to create views, frames, and constructs in an attempt to grasp evolving generative systems. The present moment of peril can be taken as an impetus and inspiration to engage with an exciting process of learning and problem solving that some call the living paradigm. This paradigm, which is still incubating in fields as diverse as architecture and design, agriculture, archaeology, restoration, and theology, is ripe for grass roots syncreses across outdated fields of knowledge. When you learn to cooperate with the last hundreds of millions of years of evolution while pursuing space age ways of averting asteroid collision, you will be prepared to lead your species toward sustainability and to make room for rapid human adaptation that restores evolution. Welcome to the One Life..

www.ingramcontent.com/pod-product-compliance
Lightning Source LLC
Chambersburg PA
CBHW071510170626
46811CB00007B/2801